The WORRY Website

Jacqueline Wilson

Illustrated by Nick Sharratt

Corgi Yearling Books

THE STORY OF TRACY BEAKER and THE WORRY WEBSITE
A CORGI YEARLING BOOK 978 0 440 86735 5 (from January 2007)
0 440 86735 5

This edition first published in Great Britain for Scholastic by Corgi Yearling,
an imprint of Random House Children s Books, 2005

1 3 5 7 9 10 8 6 4 2

THE STORY OF TRACY BEAKER
First published in Great Britain in 1991 by Doubleday,
Corgi Yearling edition published 1992
Copyright © Jacqueline Wilson, 1991
Illustrations copyright © Nick Sharratt, 1991

THE WORRY WEBSITE
First published in Great Britain in 2002 by Doubleday,
Corgi Yearling edition published 2003
Copyright © Jacqueline Wilson, 2002
Lisa's Worry Copyright © Lauren Roberts, 2002
Illustrations copyright © Nick Sharratt, 1991

Papers used by Random House Children s Books are natural, recyclable
products made from wood grown in sustainable forests. The manufacturing
processes conform to the environmental regulations of the country of origin.

Corgi Yearling Books are published by Random House Children s Books,
61–63 Uxbridge Road, London W5 5SA,
a division of The Random House Group Ltd,
in Australia by Random House Australia (Pty) Ltd,
20 Alfred Street, Milsons Point, Sydney, NSW 2061, Australia,
in New Zealand by Random House New Zealand Ltd,
18 Poland Road, Glenfield, Auckland 10, New Zealand,
and in South Africa by Random House (Pty) Ltd,
Isle of Houghton, Corner Boundary Road & Carse O Gowrie,
Houghton 2198, South Africa

THE RANDOM HOUSE GROUP Limited Reg. No. 954009
www.kidsatrandomhouse.co.uk

A CIP catalogue record for this book is available from the British Library.

Printed and bound in Great Britain by
Cox & Wyman Ltd, Reading, Berkshire

To Katie, Rhiannon and Alice

HOLLY'S WORRY

Type in your worry:

OK.

I think I'm going to get a stepmother.

There are lots of stepmothers in my favourite book of fairy tales. Don't go, 'Yuck, boring!' Fairy tales are seriously cool, *much* scarier than any X-rated video you've ever secretly watched at a sleepover. Snow White's stepmother is the scariest of all.

She doesn't *look* scary. She looks beautiful in the picture in my book – though her long queen's robes are spoilt because Hannah tried to colour them with purple wax crayon. I was FURIOUS. I felt like snapping the book shut and smacking Hannah round the head with it, even though she's only little and didn't *mean* to spoil the picture.

I minded so because it's such a special book. It used to be our mum's when she was a little girl. She gave it to me. Snow White's mum died when she was born so she got this stepmother who looked so lovely that her magic mirror said she was fairest of them all. But she was evil and mean and dead jealous when the mirror said Snow White was the fairest now, so the stepmother tried to have her chopped into bits and then she poisoned her with an apple and she fell down dead and was kept in a glass coffin until a handsome prince came by (*yawn!*) and brought her back to life. The wicked stepmother was so maddened that she boiled with rage and her shoes stayed so red hot she couldn't take them off and she had to dance until she died.

She must have had awful blisters. I've got one

where my old trainers are rubbing. Dad doesn't always get it together when we need new shoes. It's not his fault he's so busy. Yes it is. I'm not making excuses for my dad any more. I can't stick him now. And I especially can't stick *her*.

I'm going to add to my worry.

I wish she was wicked.

That sounds daft. Mr Speed will think I'm seriously weird. Mind you, Mr Speed is a little bit weird himself. He's speedy, like his name. He whizzes up and down the school corridors, he dodges round the desks in the classroom, and he skips across the playground. He really *did* skip once when Claire brought a skipping rope to school. He could do all sorts of fancy footwork too – but then he tripped and fell over and said a *very* rude word. He's not a bit like the other teachers.

This Worry Website is all his idea. It's instead of Circle Time. You know, when you all sit in a circle, fidgeting, and you're meant to discuss your problems. Sometimes it's dead boring because someone like Samantha bangs on about missing her dad. Everyone always feels sorry for Samantha because she's so little and pretty with lovely long fair hair. Even Mr Speed has a special smiley way of looking at her that makes me sick.

Sometimes Circle Time is terribly embarrassing because someone stupid like poor William confides the sort of problem that should stay a deadly secret. He told the whole class that he wets the bed and his dad yells at him and makes him cry and his mum says she can't keep up with washing his sopping sheets. Some of the kids giggled and poor William looked as if he was going to cry again. Mr Speed got *very* fierce with the gigglers and praised William for being so honest and sensible over a tiny physical problem that happens to heaps of people – but even Mr Speed couldn't stop half the class calling poor William 'Wetty Willie' in the playground.

So maybe that's why he came up with the Worry Website idea.

'I've designed the super-cool, wacky, wicked website on the classroom computer, OK? Any time any of you have a problem then access the Worry Website when it's your turn on the computer and type it in. You don't need to put your name. Then we can all contribute our comments and suggestions – make them *kind* and *constructive* or I'll leap up and down on you in my Doc Martens, get it?'

We got it.

Everyone started typing in their worries. Someone had a good long moan about their sneaky sister and their brainy brother.

Someone was worried about being bottom of the class.

Someone wrote about having scary nightmares.

Someone was sad because their pet rat had just died.

One of the boys wrote that he liked one of the girls a lot. That made everyone giggle – and Greg went very pink. Hmm! I wonder who he fancies?

Someone else went on and on. *Oh boo hoo, it's so sad, I miss my dad, etc, etc.* We all know who *that* was. At least Samantha can still see her dad when she goes to stay with him and his new girlfriend.

Well, I see my mum. Sometimes. I have to take my little sister Hannah so she can get to know our mum. She left when Hannah was just a baby. Mum had Depression which made her very sad so she cried a lot and then ran off. When she ran off I guess Dad and Hannah and I got Depression too because we all felt very sad and cried a lot as well. It felt very scary when Dad cried so I told him that it was OK. *I'd* look after him and Hannah now.

I do look after both of them. I've been almost like

11

Hannah's mum. When she was a baby I fed her and washed her and dressed her and changed her (yucky, but you have to do it). I cuddled her lots and played peek-a-boo and do you know something? The very first word she said was Holly. That's my name.

She's said millions and millions and millions of words since. She is a total chatterbox. She's in the Reception class at my school and Miss Morgan obviously adores her – though she always gets into trouble for talking. She even talks during Story Time. She doesn't mean to be naughty. She just likes to join in.

I read to her at bedtime from my special book of fairy tales. She likes 'Red Riding Hood' best, especially the wolf bits. 'Oh, Grandma, what big teeth you've got,' I say in a teeny-tiny Red Riding Hood voice and then Hannah shrieks, 'All the better to EAT YOU ALL UP!' and bounces up out of bed at me, gnashing her teeth. Once she bit me on the nose by accident. She can be a very boisterous baby sister.

My favourite fairy tale is 'Snow White'. When I read the start of the story out loud and say that Snow White's hair is as black as coal and her skin as white as snow and her lips as red as berries, Hannah always shouts, '*Holly* berries!' and stabs at the picture with her finger.

'That's you, Holly,' she says.

I wish! I don't look the slightest bit like Snow White. I *have* got red lips (especially if I've been eating red Smarties) but I often have a red nose too (I get lots of colds). My hair is straggly mouse (though my *nails* are sometimes as black as coal). Snow White is as pretty as a picture. *Her* picture in the book is beautiful, with tiny glass mirrors and red apples all round the border and Snow White herself is wearing a white dress embroidered all over with tiny gold stars. Snow White is small too, not that much bigger than the Seven Dwarves, and she's thin as a pin. I am not pretty. I am as plain as an empty page and a bit on the podgy side too.

I don't care. I take after my dad. I used to be glad. I used to love my dad *sooooooo* much. Whenever he collects us from the After School Club he always says, 'Where are my special girlfriends?' I have always been his Big Grown-up Girlfriend and Hannah his Teeny Tiny Girlfriend. But now Dad has a real girlfriend. I'm scared she's going to come and live with us and be my stepmother and it's not fair.

'Yes, it is so fair,' said Hannah. 'We *want* her to be our mother.'

'No, we've *got* a mother already. You remember, Hannah,' I said.

'Not really,' said Hannah.

We haven't gone on a visit to our mum for quite a while. We *want* to, but the last time we didn't get on with Mum's new boyfriend, Mike.

'Oh yes! He shouted and we cried,' said Hannah.

'You cried. I'm not a baby,' I said.

'You did so cry, I saw. I don't like that Mike. *Or* our mum,' said Hannah.

'Yes you do,' I insisted.

'No, I like our *new* mum much, much, much more,' said Hannah.

You will never guess who this new mum is going to be. Miss Morgan. Yes, *that* Miss Morgan. Hannah's teacher.

'I love her to bits,' said Hannah happily.

Dad loves her to bits too.

I suppose I used to like her just a little bit myself. I used to take Hannah into her classroom every morning. Dad has to drop us off at school very early or else he'll be late for work. Miss Morgan is always there though. I used to like seeing what she was wearing. She doesn't look a bit like a teacher. She's got long hair way past her shoulders and she wears long dresses too, all bright and embroidered, and she has these purple suede pointy boots with high heels. She looks as if she's stepped straight out of my fairy-story book.

I liked the way her Reception classroom looked too. It was all so bright and cosy and small. I'd hang about for a while, keeping an eye on Hannah, showing her the water trough and the giant building bricks and the powder paints and the playhouse. I especially loved the playhouse. I hadn't had much time for playing since Hannah was born. I

suddenly wanted to scrunch up small and squeeze in through the tiny door and squat safe inside, too little to do anything else but play.

I didn't, of course. I'm not daft like poor William. But Miss Morgan saw me staring, and the next day when I dropped Hannah off she asked me if I'd be sweet enough to tidy up the dolls and the little beds and tables and chairs because all those four-year-olds had got them all higgledy-piggledy.

I sighed a bit, like I didn't really want to, and then I leant through the open window of the playhouse and sorted it all out. It was kind of fun. I don't know why. Doing it for real is no fun at all. Still, the playhouse dolls didn't whine or fidget or refuse to put their arms in their cardie like *someone* I could mention.

The next morning Miss Morgan said, 'Guess what, Holly, the playhouse is in a mess *again*.' I sighed and said, 'I suppose you want me to fix it?' – and so it got to be a habit. I also put fresh water in the trough and cleaned up the sandpit and tested out the building bricks to see if there were enough to make a proper fairy-tale palace like the pictures in my book. Hannah didn't join in these early morning games. She just wriggled onto Miss Morgan's lap and chattered to her non-stop.

'Feel free to tip her off your lap whenever you get tired. She does tend to go on and on,' I said.

Miss Morgan didn't seem to mind a bit. I sometimes wished I could climb on her lap and chatter too, just like Hannah. Miss Morgan used to be my favourite teacher in the school – even better than Mr Speed.

Dad met Mr Speed and Miss Morgan when he came to Parents' Evening. Dad said that Mr Speed was very pleased with my progress and that he said I was a very good, sensible girl and the little star of his class. I twinkled. Dad said that Miss Morgan was very pleased with Hannah too and that she said she was very lively and loving. If Miss Morgan had said Hannah was very good or sensible she would be a terrible fibber.

'Mr Speed's smashing, isn't he, Dad?' I said happily.

'Yes he is,' said Dad. 'Miss Morgan's rather special too, isn't she?'

Dad took to coming into Hannah's class with us every morning even though it made him late for work. Then Miss Morgan came round to our house with some special wax crayons for Hannah (big mistake: remember Snow White's stepmother's purple robe) and some rainbow metallic pens for me. The next Saturday, surprise surprise, we just happened to bump into Miss Morgan in the children's library. We all chatted for a bit and then we took Hannah to the swings and *then* we all had lunch in McDonald's. Before we knew what was happening we were seeing Miss Morgan every single Saturday and sometimes Sundays too.

I didn't mind a bit at first. I know this makes me the most seriously stupid, dumb dolthead but there you are. Even poor William would have twigged what was going on – but I thought Miss Morgan was *my* friend. And Hannah's too, of course. I didn't *dream* that she was there because of our dad.

Miss Morgan is as pretty as a princess. Our dad doesn't look a bit like a handsome prince. Well, not the ones in my fairy-tale book. They don't wear baggy T-shirts and tracksuit bottoms and fluffy socks with holes in the toes. Though Dad got all dressed up in a suit on Friday night.

'I'm going out, girls. I've asked Auntie Evie up the road to babysit.'

'We don't need Auntie Evie. She fusses too much,' I said, pulling a face. '*I'll* babysit for Hannah, Dad.'

'I know you're just like a little mother to Hannah, love, but I'd feel happier if Auntie Evie was here to keep an eye on things,' said Dad, tying the knot in the funny *Simpsons* tie Hannah and I gave him last birthday. He only wears his tie if he's going somewhere really special.

'Are you going out somewhere posh with your mates from work, Dad?' I asked.

'No, love,' said Dad, sprucing his hair in the mirror. 'Why does it always stick straight up?'

'Maybe you need some hair gel, Dad.'

He peered in the mirror, his head at an odd angle. 'You don't think I'm going thin on top, do you, Holly?'

'Yeah, like you're almost totally bald,' I said, teasing him. 'Leave it out, Dad, you've got lovely thick hair.'

'You're a great little kid, Holly,' said Dad, giving me a hug.

'So where *are* you going, Dad?'

Dad looked in the mirror rather than at me. 'I'm taking Jenny out for a meal.'

'Jenny?'

Dad went red.

'You know. Miss Morgan.'

I stared at him. Hannah bounced up.

'A meal? Can we come too? Can we go to McDonald's?' Hannah begged.

'No, no, you wouldn't want to come, Hannah. We're going to this Italian place.'

'I like Italian food. I like spaghetti,' Hannah insisted.

'Well, maybe you and Holly can come with us another time. But this is a meal just for grown-ups,' said Dad.

'It's a *date*,' I said. I spat the word out as if it was deadly poison. 'You and Miss Morgan. You're going *out* with her!'

'You don't mind, do you?' said Dad. 'You *like* Jenny – Miss Morgan.'

'We *love* her,' said Hannah. 'Oh, Dad, is she your girlfriend now?'

'Well . . . sort of,' said Dad, positively beetroot.

'Oh great, great, great!' Hannah shouted. 'Here Dad, why don't you marry Miss Morgan and then she can be our mum!'

'Not so fast, Teeny Tiny Girlfriend,' said Dad, and he picked Hannah up and swung her round and round. Her feet flew out and her left Pokémon slipper clunked me straight on the head.

I made a lot of fuss though my head didn't really hurt a bit. It was inside me that was hurting. My dad – and Miss Morgan!

'What's up, Big Grown-up Girlfriend?' said Dad. 'Is your head really sore? Shall I kiss it better?'

'I'm not a baby. Don't be so daft,' I snapped. 'Save your kissing for Miss Morgan.'

Dad looked like I'd thrown a bucket of cold water all over him. He blinked at me.

'I thought you'd be dead chuffed like Hannah,' he said. 'You *like* Jenny, Holly. I don't get it.'

I didn't really get it either. I just knew it was all spoilt now. And *I* carried on spoiling it. We still went out every Saturday, but I mucked it up. I sighed and fussed and moaned in the children's library. Whenever Miss Morgan picked out some book she thought I might enjoy I'd glance at it and give a big yawn and go, 'Boring!' So she found picture books for Hannah instead. Dad and Miss Morgan sat squashed together on one of those silly saggy cushion chairs, with Hannah tucked under their chins looking at the pictures in the book. They looked like a real family already.

The girl behind the counter in McDonald's thought they were a family too. Hannah jumped up and said she wanted a giant portion of French fries and *five* ice creams and the girl laughed and looked at Miss Morgan and said, 'Perhaps we'd better ask Mum first.'

'She's not our mum,' I said fiercely. When we sat down with our food I thumped my plastic tray so hard my milk shake tipped and trickled all over me, and quite a bit of Miss Morgan too.

'For goodness' sake, Holly, what's the matter with you?' said Dad, mopping at Miss Morgan with his paper napkin. He just let me drip. 'You're behaving like a total idiot.'

'You're the total idiot,' I muttered. Not softly enough.

'I've just about had enough of you, showing me up and behaving so badly,' Dad hissed.

'Here, Holly, let's go to the Ladies' and get some paper towels,' said Miss Morgan in a friendly but very firm teacher's voice, so I couldn't quite manage to say no. When we were in the Ladies' she didn't mess around with the milk-shake stains. She put her hands on my shoulders and looked me straight in the eyes.

'It's OK, Holly. I understand the way you feel.'

'No, you don't,' I said sulkily.

I didn't see how she could understand when *I* didn't have a clue why I felt so bad and was acting bad into the bargain.

'I like your dad – and he seems to like me,' said Miss Morgan.

'Yuck!' I said.

'Yes, OK, it seems very yucky to you. It probably would to me too if I was in the same situation.'

The *really* yucky thing was she was being so nicey-nicey-nice to me, *sooooo* soft and sweet. It made me feel fiercer than ever.

'I promise you, I'm not trying to take the place of your mum. I know just how much she means to you. She'll always stay your mum – and Hannah's – for ever and ever, even though you don't see her any more.'

'We do *so* see her!' I shouted. 'We see her lots and lots and lots, so you can just shut up and stay away from me and my family.'

I rushed into a cubicle and locked the door and wouldn't come out for ages. In fact *Dad* had to come into the Ladies' to get me out and it was dead embarrassing and everyone was staring.

I managed to hold things in until I was in bed that night and then I cried and cried and cried. I tried to cry quietly but I woke Hannah.

'Are you crying because you've been so bad?' she whispered. She had been awestruck by my behaviour.

'I'm *not* crying. I've just got a cold,' I snuffled, blowing my nose.

I really did get a cold the next day and I made such a fuss that Dad let me stay off school. Auntie Evie up the road came to keep an eye on me. When she dozed off watching *Neighbours* after lunch I crept into the hall and made a phone call – to my mum.

Mum didn't know who I was at first.

Well, she *did*. She just didn't recognize my voice and said, 'Who?' suspiciously as if it was someone playing a joke on her.

'It's *me*, Mum.' I paused. I wondered if I was going to have to add, '*You* know. Holly. Your *daughter*.'

'What do you want, Holly? Is something wrong?'

'No. Yes. It's Dad.'

'Well, what about him? He's not ill, is he? Because I can't really have you girls to stay at the moment as

I'm not too great myself and I'm having all sorts of dramas with Mike and . . .'

She went on and on and on. Then she remembered.

'Anyway. What about your dad?'

'He's got a *girlfriend*!'

'Has he?' She sounded so casual, as if I'd just announced he'd got a new tie.

'She's a teacher at our school.'

'Oh well. That figures. It's the only way your dad would ever meet anyone.'

I hated the way Mum always sounded so sniffy about Dad, like he was the most boring man on earth.

'Don't you mind, Mum?'

'Well, what's it got to do with me?'

'It's serious. She might end up our stepmother.'

'Oh! Isn't she very nice to you then?'

'She's . . .' I couldn't quite tell an outright lie. 'She's OK.'

'Then what are you worried about, eh?'

'Well, she *could* turn out horrid. Most stepmothers are. Like in "Snow White".'

'Ah. "Snow White". I had that fairy-tale book when I was a little girl.'

'I *know*. You gave it to me.'

I can't stand it when Mum forgets things. Sometimes it feels as if she's forgotten all about me. I wanted to tell her how much I loved her and missed her but the words wouldn't sort themselves out and while I was still wondering how to say it Mum said, 'Well, I've got to go now, Holly. See you. Bye.'

So I put the phone down. I stopped feeling I loved her and hated her for a bit. She said 'see you' but she doesn't want to. She doesn't even like talking to me on the phone much now.

Dad says it's because she feels bad about leaving us. I think maybe *she's* bad.

I take after her now.

I went back to school the next day because it was dead depressing staying at home. My nose was sniffier than ever and so was I. Samantha was showing off her new hair slides, which were like little butterflies, but I simply yawned and said they looked stupid. Samantha said I was just jealous because she had long fair curls  and I didn't. I said I didn't care one bit about having long fair curls. (*Big* lie.) Greg said he didn't think long fair curls were all that great and he much preferred *my* hair! Old Greg is going as daft as poor William if you ask me.

Mr Speed told me to hand the marked homework out and asked me to read aloud to the others and sent me with a message to the Head. I bashed the homework books bang on the desks, I read aloud in a bored, flat, can't-be-bothered voice, and I dawdled down the corridor so slowly after giving my message I missed half the lesson.

'I wonder why you're in such a bad mood today, Holly?' said Mr Speed.

I shrugged and pouted. Mr Speed imitated me. He looked so funny I very nearly gave in and giggled.

'Maybe you need a bit of peace and quiet? I know! How about a little computer practice?'

I knew this was a Crafty Ploy. Mr Speed wanted me to access his Worry Website. And I couldn't resist. I typed it in. Remember?

I think I'm going to get a stepmother.

I wish she was wicked.

Comments:

You're nuts!

What is she on about?

How do you know the person with the worry is a girl?

Because it's such a silly girly thing.

You're being dead sexist.

Look, what about his/her PROBLEM?

What problem? Heaps of kids get stepmothers. I've got one and she's OK.

I've got a mum and a dad and a stepmum and a stepdad and it's great at Christmas and birthdays because you get two lots of presents.

Why do you want a WICKED stepmother???

I've GOT a wicked stepmother. You can have mine!

I didn't think these comments particularly kind. Or constructive. There were other even more useless suggestions that I deleted. I sat staring at the screen, wishing I could delete myself. Mr Speed saw me and whizzed right over before I could quit the website.

'Aha! So you're having a peep at the Worry Website, Holly. Hmm. Interesting worry! Have you typed in your comment for this poor soul who wants a wicked stepmother?'

He was trying to kid me that the website is ultra-anonymous. But I'm not daft. I gave him a long hard look.

'I'm the poor soul, Mr Speed. You know it's me.'

'Yes, that's very true, Holly. You've caught me out.'

'*You* haven't put a comment.'

'That's also true. OK.' He leaned over me and typed.

I don't know WHY you want a wicked stepmother. Perhaps you can elaborate?

He waited. I fidgeted.

'Elaborate means tell me more,' said Mr Speed.

'I know. I don't know *how* though. It's all muddly. It's my dad – and Miss Morgan.'

Mr Speed's eyes opened wide.

'*Our* Miss Morgan?'

'This is highly confidential, Mr Speed,' I said hurriedly.

'Mum's the word,' said Mr Speed, finger on his lips.

So I told him. His eyes got wider and wider, like the dog in the fairy tale with eyes as big as dinner plates.

'Your dad's a very lucky man,' he said eventually. 'And I should imagine young Hannah's thrilled. So . . . how do you feel, Holly?'

'I feel bad,' I said. 'And I keep acting bad and then I feel even worse. And Miss Morgan is always so nicey-nicey-nice about it. I want *her* to be bad. If she was really wicked like Snow White's stepmother then I could hate her and be horrid to her and it would be perfectly OK.'

'I can't *quite* imagine Miss Morgan trying to force you to eat poisoned apples,' said Mr Speed. 'Let alone hiring an axeman to chop you into little bits in the middle of the forest.'

'I think I've got a worry that can't be solved,' I said gloomily.

'Well . . . we could just fiddle with the meaning of wicked. I've always thought Miss Morgan an ultra-lovely, delightful young woman – this is also highly confidential, Holly. I especially admire her amazing purple boots. We could well say she looks seriously wicked. Right?'

I groaned.

'Sorry!' Mr Speed shook his head at me apologetically. 'I'll work on it. But there aren't always easy answers to worries. You know that. Tell you something though. You're *not* bad. You're still my little star. You'll get your twinkle back soon, you'll see.'

I kept out of Miss Morgan's way that week. I delivered Hannah off at the door of the Reception class but didn't go in myself. Dad went out with Miss Morgan on Friday night but he came home early when I was still sitting up in bed reading my fairy-tale book. He popped his head round the door to tell me to put the light off and go to sleep. He seemed all sad and scowly. Maybe he'd had a row with Miss Morgan!

However, she came round to our house on Saturday looking extra-specially lovely in a long purple dress with little mirrors all round the hem.

'Let me see if I can see my face,' said Hannah, kneeling down and peering into each mirror. 'Mirror, mirror, on the wall, who is the fairest of them all?'

'Mirror, mirror on her skirt, who is acting like a stupid little squirt?' I said, yanking Hannah upright.

'Ouch! You're so grumpy now, Holly. I don't want you to come round the town with us because you spoil everything,' said Hannah.

'Good, I don't *want* to come,' I said, but I felt bad, bad, bad. My eyes went all watery because even Hannah didn't want me any more.

'I think we won't *all* go round the town today,'

said Miss Morgan. Her eyes were as glittery as the little mirrors on her skirt. 'Maybe Holly and I might just go shopping together?'

'What about *me*?' said Hannah indignantly.

'I'll take you to the library and the swings, Hannah, and then we'll have an ice cream or two – or three or four or five – in McDonald's, OK?' said Dad.

Hannah had her mouth open to protest bitterly but she got sidetracked by the ice-cream bribe. Maybe my mouth was open too. I didn't get what was going on.

'I don't want to go shopping,' I said.

'Yes, you do – if you've got money in your pocket,' said Dad, and he handed me a ten-pound note.

I couldn't believe it. Ten pounds, all for me! So I sloped off with Miss Morgan. I decided I wasn't going to speak to her though. Not one word, all the way into town. But the weird thing was, she didn't say one word to me either! She just strode along in her purple pointy boots and whenever I glanced at her she *glared* at me. I'd never seen her glare before, not even when Hannah's Reception class got really, really rowdy and started throwing powder paint about. (It might have been Hannah who started it because she ended

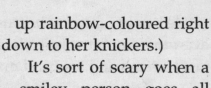

up rainbow-coloured right down to her knickers.)

It's sort of scary when a smiley person goes all glarey. The silence was starting to get on my nerves so much that I blurted out, 'I want to go to Claire's Accessories to get some of those little butterfly slides. And maybe one of those little lucky-bead bracelets.'

Miss Morgan sniffed. 'You're lucky all right, Holly. Your dad spoils you so. And you've certainly been acting like a spoilt brat recently. I'm getting sick of it.'

I stared at her. It was as if she'd suddenly started spitting toads.

'You're not supposed to talk to me like that. You're a *teacher*!'

'And I'm also your dad's girlfriend and if you'd only give us a chance I think we'd be really happy together. But you just want to muck everything up, don't you? Can't you see how unhappy you're making your dad?'

'He's only unhappy because of *you*. *You've* mucked everything up. It was really great before, when it was just Hannah and Dad and me.'

'*You* felt great,' said Miss Morgan, and she stamped her boot so that her skirt swung and all the little mirrors glittered. 'Don't you realize how *lonely* your dad felt?'

'He wasn't a bit lonely! And anyway, maybe – maybe my mum might come back and then he'd have *her*, wouldn't he?'

'You know perfectly well your mum isn't ever going to come back. And even if she did your dad wouldn't want her. She walked out on all of you, even little Hannah. I don't see how she could ever have done that. Why do you act like she's so wonderful when she could do a wicked thing like leave her own children?'

'*You're* wicked and I hate you! I wish you'd stomp off in your silly boots and never ever come back!' Tears spilled down my cheeks. 'Why did you have to turn out so horrible?'

'Oh, Holly!' said Miss Morgan. Tears streamed down her cheeks too. 'I'm sorry. I *am* wicked. I don't want to be horrible. I can't do this any more. It's awful. I like you too much.'

'No you don't! No-one does. No-one wants me!'

'I want you very, very much,' she said.

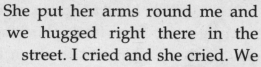

She put her arms round me and we hugged right there in the street. I cried and she cried. We kept on hugging. I sniffled so much I dripped on her purple dress but she didn't mind a bit. She found her hankie and I blew my nose and she blew her nose too and then we went off to this posh coffee shop and had wonderful grown-up frothy coffee and an apple Danish pastry each. I had difficulty eating mine at first because I had hiccups from all that crying. Miss Morgan saw me hesitating.

'They're not poisoned apples, I promise,' she said.

I peered at her suspiciously, spooning up the froth from my coffee.

'What's Mr Speed been saying to you?'

'Mr Speed?' said Miss Morgan, dead nonchalant. She shook her head, tossing her lovely long hair over her shoulder. 'Oh, nothing in particular.'

You know what teachers are like. They always back each other up.

I think Mr Speed *might* have told her my Worry, even though it's supposed to be confidential. He was just trying to act like a fairy godmother and grant my wish. I had a sudden vision of Mr Speed in a fairy frock clutching a wand and I laughed so much I blew the rest of my froth off my coffee.

'What?' said Miss Morgan, giggling a bit too.

'Oh, nothing in particular,' I said. I thought for a bit. 'Miss Morgan – I'm sorry I said all that stuff. I don't really hate you.'

'I'm sorry too, Holly. I didn't mean all that stuff I said either. I was just feeling fed up and worried because your dad said on Friday that we might have to stop seeing each other if it was making you so unhappy. He always puts you and Hannah first.'

'Well . . . you come second,' I said, patting her hand. 'And I'll tell Dad I don't really want you two to break up.'

'Yes, you might end up with a *really* wicked stepmother,' said Miss Morgan, and she pulled this dreadful frowny ferocious face.

I laughed and she laughed – and we both knew we'd kind of made friends. They never seem to do that in fairy stories, do they? Then we

went shopping and I bought Miss Morgan a little comb for her long thick hair and I got Dad some gel for his short thinning hair. I found some butterfly slides but I bought them for Hannah. I chose special little gold star slides for me. Miss Morgan said they really, really suited me.

I wore them to school on Monday and Greg said they looked lovely and Mr Speed said I seemed to be twinkling splendidly. He had a twinkle in *his* eye too.

Miss Morgan said she's going to make Hannah and me special dresses. Hannah's is going to have little mirrors and mine is going to have stars embroidered all over.

I suppose they could just be bridesmaid's dresses . . .

GREG'S WORRY

Type in your worry:

Oh dear. I hope no-one's looking. This is so embarrassing. OK. Here goes.

I like this girl. I like her very much. I want to be her friend. I want to be her BOYfriend. I've gone all red and shuddery and yucky just typing it! I hate all this lovey-dovey stuff. It really sucks. I don't WANT to feel like this. I generally HATE girls.

I certainly hate my sister Sarah-Jane. She is only a year younger than me but she's little and dinky-looking and she talks in a special lispy baby voice so that everyone treats her like she's five years old.

It's so irritating having a *little* sister. She's allowed to kick me or elbow me in the ribs or creep up behind me and pinch my neck but if I clump her one I'm in serious trouble. I'm *generally* in serious trouble at home about Sarah-Jane.

She's so sneaky too. She puts on this little simper and says, 'Mum, I don't want to be mean and tell on Greg, but—' and then she *does* tell. She exaggerates like crazy. And then Mum bellows, 'Gregory!' and I know I'm for it. I *hate* being called Gregory. It's a saint's name. You certainly need the patience of a saint with Sarah-Jane as your sister.

I don't like my girl cousins much either, Yvonne and Julia and Katrina. They come round our house on a Sunday and they all squeeze into Sarah-Jane's bedroom and try on each other's clothes and do each other's hair. They do this for *hours*. Then I have to sit with them for Sunday lunch and they go whisper, whisper, whisper, giggle, giggle, giggle. It is *torture*. I feel so tense about it that I can't eat comfortably and that makes me do certain rude

windy things and then they all squeal and Mum goes, 'Gregory!' as if I'm doing it on purpose. Which just occasionally I am.

I didn't reckon any of the girls in my class at school either. Well, Claire's OK because she's good at football and I suppose I've always thought Samantha's ever so pretty – but she reminds me too much of Sarah-Jane. I never really noticed any of the other girls.

But then I got to sit behind Holly when we all went into Mr Speed's class. I stuck my feet on the back of her chair and kicked a bit, because that's what you *do* when a girl sits in front of you. Most of them whine and fidget and moan that you're getting mud on their skirt. But Holly whipped round quick as a wink, her fingers went fiddly-flick – and there were my shoelaces tied together! Then she gave me this great grin. I couldn't help grinning back even though she'd tied such a tight knot I couldn't pick it open and had to saw through my shoelaces with my penknife.

I don't know how to put it into words. It was just her big grin. It really got to me.

So I tried to figure out ways of making her grin again. The next day I came to school wearing my muddy walks-in-the-country welly boots. We don't often *go* for muddy walks in the country so they'd got a bit small without my realizing. I had to scrunch up my toes, which was dead uncomfortable. I also had to put up with everyone asking me why I was wearing my wellies when it wasn't raining. Not so much as a cloud in the sky.

Mr Speed did this whole pantomime thing of putting up an imaginary umbrella. Everyone laughed. Holly laughed too. I waited until everyone stopped sniggering at my boring foot-blistering boots. Mr Speed started telling some soppy fairy story in the Literacy Hour and Holly was listening hard, her hair tucked behind her neat little ears. *Then* I put my boots on the back of her chair.

She turned round.

I waited. I thought she'd see she couldn't tie any laces this time and give that glorious grin again. But she sighed, stiffened her hand, and gave the tip of each boot a swift karate chop.

 It was such AGONY on my poor rubbed tootsies that I screamed. 'Oh my goodness, Greg!' Mr Speed exploded, clutching his chest. 'You'll give me a heart attack. I hope you have a totally convincing excuse for that banshee wail. Are you being fiendishly attacked by invisible aliens?'

'No, Mr Speed,' I mumbled, trying to ease my throbbing feet.

'Then why the scream? Is it National Torment Mr Speed Day today? No, that's *every* day as far as you lot are concerned. I warn you, children, I am in a very savage mood today. I am becoming more savage every second, moodier every minute. Well, Greg, I'm waiting for your explanation. I've given you long enough to concoct one. Were you perhaps provoked in some way?'

'No, Mr Speed,' I said firmly. 'I was just messing about.'

Holly turned round and gave me a quick smile, an abbreviated text-message version of her gorgeous grin.

I'd have listened to Mr Speed lecturing me all day long just for that one weeny glance.

But it didn't get me anywhere.

I tried coming to school in my bedroom slippers the next day. My poor sore feet needed a little bit of cosseting. Unfortunately *this* time it decided to rain. In fact it positively poured buckets and my slippers got sodden.

I had to lie down on my back at the side of the classroom and rest both soaking slippers on the radiators until they steamed. Mr Speed came in late and pretended to trip right over me.

'I've always assumed that standard classroom posture is bottom on chair. Is there any reason why you prefer this lying-on-back, legs-in-air position, Greg?' Mr Speed said wearily.

I told him I was simply trying to dry out my slippers.

'Ah, I wondered what that extraordinary smell was,' said Mr Speed. 'Feet *off* the radiator, please! You'll give yourself chilblains as well as stinking the

place out. I'm beginning to find your inappropriate footwear fetish rather irritating, lad. I suggest you turn up in standard sensible shoes tomorrow or you *might* just find yourself left behind in the classroom when we go off on the school trip.'

The school trip! It wasn't anything to get excited about in itself. We were just going to a musty old museum. But we travelled there by coach! I had to find some way of sitting next to Holly on the journey.

She's got lots and lots and lots of friends in our class, but she hasn't got one *particular* friend. I was in with a chance. But she could pick anyone. There are thirty children in our class so she could have her choice of twenty-nine of us.

I wondered *how* I could get her to pick me.

I sauntered past the computer dead casually and then looked at my worry on the website to see if anyone had given me any good tips about getting a girlfriend.

Ha ha ha. I am not laughing. I am being extremely sarcastic. There weren't any tips at all, just a whole load of rubbish.

Comments:

I hate girls too.

So do I. They've got such silly squeaky voices that they make your head ache when they go on at you. And they don't understand important stuff like football.

Oh yes they do! I bet I know who you are and you're lousy at football. I don't want to boast but I'm in the football team even though I'm a girl and I scored three goals last match so you shut up.

See! They go on at you! You've proved my point.

I bet none of the girls in our class would go out with any of the boys because the boys are all so childish and stupid. I hate BOYS.

Some of the boys are OK. I would like one boy in particular to be my boyfriend. Guess who I am!

My heart leapt when I read that one, but this person had added her name at the end. Not her full name because we're not allowed to. So she put S——————a.

Well, even weird William would have no trouble at all working that one out.

'Aha!' said Mr Speed, peering over my shoulder.

I felt my cheeks burning, as if someone had switched on an electric fire in my face. My glasses steamed up so I could hardly see.

'This is a daft worry,' I said quickly. 'I don't

know what sort of idiot would write that.'

'*My* sort of idiot,' said Mr Speed. He scrolled through the answers. 'Oh dear! They're not very sympathetic, are they? I'd hoped they might have some kind of constructive advice for this poor lovelorn chap. *I* need advice.'

'Are you in love, Mr Speed?' I asked, astonished. I mean, Mr Speed is a *teacher*. And he's old too. Well, I think he is. It's difficult to tell with grown-ups. It's easy enough to tell whether a kid is five or ten or fifteen – but how do I know whether Mr Speed is twenty-five or thirty or thirty-five or even *older*.

'Don't stare at me like that, lad. I'm not ready for my pension yet,' said Mr Speed sharply.

'How do you read people's minds, Mr Speed?' I said.

'Oh, it's my laser-light bionic glasses,' said Mr Speed, wrinkling his nose so that his glasses wiggled about.

I laughed and wiggled my own glasses back.

'Mr Speed, do you think girls mind if boys wear glasses?' I said.

'I don't think they mind a bit,' said Mr Speed. He struck a silly pose. 'I've never found it a deterrent.'

'But you're having problems now, Mr Speed?

'Indeed I am, Greg. In the presence of a certain lady I go all red and shuddery and yucky, to quote these expressive words on the website.'

'And do you think this lady will be your girlfriend, Mr Speed?'

'Alas and alack, her heart belongs to another,' said Mr Speed. 'So *my* heart is broken!' He thumped himself on the chest and  groaned. He didn't *mean* it. He's always carrying on like that. He's a bit nuts if you ask me.

'*However,*' Mr Speed said, with emphasis, 'the lovelorn boy with the current worry on the website should not be downhearted. It looks like his lovely little lady friend is making it particularly plain that she cares for him.'

I blinked. I backtracked through his speech. He talks in such a funny way that this is necessary sometimes.

'You mean you think I – he – is in with a chance?' I said excitedly.

'Definitely. She couldn't be making it plainer. What more do you want, lad? Does she have to stand on a desktop and proclaim her love to the entire class?'

I thought about it.

'I'd quite like that,' I said.

'Mmm, so would I!' said Mr Speed, laughing. 'But I don't think she'll be quite as bold as all that.'

'So you think she'd maybe sit next to this boy on the school trip?'

'You bet. He should just *ask* her,' said Mr Speed.

So I did.

I couldn't quite get up the courage until we were all set to go and Mr Speed was taking the register. Then I very gently nudged Holly with my shoe.

She turned round, sighed elaborately, and started undoing one of my new laces.

'Don't Holly, please! My mum will go spare. I had to nick *these* laces out of our Sarah-Jane's Irish dancing shoes.'

'Well, quit kicking me then,' Holly hissed.

'I'm not kicking, I'm attracting your attention.'

'Oh yeah?' said Holly. She looked straight into my eyes. 'Why?'

I went red and shuddery and yuckety-yucky *but* I looked straight back at her and said it. 'Will you sit next to me on the coach?'

'OK,' said Holly, like it was no big deal at all. Then she grinned.

I felt I was shooting straight through the classroom ceiling up into the bright blue sky.

Then Mr Speed told us to line up for the coach. Everyone surged forward, out of the classroom, along the corridor, out of the door, across the playground, out of the gate to where the school coach was waiting. But I hung back with Holly, grinning and grinning at her. And she grinned back.

Mr Speed was herding everyone onto the coach. He called to us to hurry up. Then he caught hold of me.

'Here's your chance, boy,' he said, and he propelled me forwards, up the big steps and onto the front seat . . . next to *Samantha*!

'Hi, Greg,' she said, smiling at me. 'I've saved this seat for you.'

I stared at her in horror.

'But I'm sitting next to—'

'Samantha!' commanded Mr Speed. He seized me by the shoulders and sat me down on the front seat beside her. 'Don't be bashful, lad,' he whispered in my ear. 'Take this golden opportunity.'

'But Mr Speed, you've got it all *wrong*,' I wailed. 'I don't *like* Samantha.'

Mr Speed was hurrying up and down the coach aisle checking on purses and packed lunches and sick bags and didn't even hear me.

But Samantha did.

She looked amazed. Then appalled. Her blue eyes went all watery. I felt horrible.

'I didn't mean I don't *like* you, Samantha. Of course I do. You're *ever* so nice, but it's just there's this other girl I like better.'

I seemed to be making it worse.

'Well, I don't like *you*,' she said. 'Get off this seat! I wouldn't sit next to you if you went down on your knees and *begged*.'

'Fat chance,' I said. I jumped up – but Mr Speed rushed past and gave me a shove down again.

'Up and down, up and down, like a jack-in-the-box,' he said. 'Sit *still*, Greg.'

'But I don't want to sit next to Samantha, Mr Speed!'

'He's certainly *not* sitting next to me!'

Mr Speed stopped, hands on hips. He breathed in deeply. This is generally a warning signal.

'Well well well! I was under

50

the impression *I* was the teacher and *you* were the pupils, but I've obviously got that entirely wrong, because here you are giving *me* the orders.' He paused ominously. 'Are you the teacher here, Gregory?'

'No, Mr Speed.'

'What about you, Samantha?'

'No, Mr Speed.'

'Then, my goodness, *I* must be the teacher. And I say sit down in your seats and do not utter another word or I will sit on you myself.'

I didn't utter a word to Samantha and she didn't utter a word to me for the entire journey. We weren't on speaking terms.

I tried kneeling on my seat to see Holly. I tried to attract Holly's attention. I failed. I attracted Mr Speed's attention instead. This was a *big* mistake.

He made me stick with him all the way round the museum, while all the others were allowed to ramble around in little groups having fun. I called after Holly but she stared straight past me as if she couldn't even see me.

'You're an exceptionally aggravating boy, Gregory,' said Mr Speed. 'Why do you have to be so fickle with your affections? First you declare undying love for Samantha and yet when I give you the opportunity to sit next to her you behave totally offensively and transfer your affections to Holly.'

'I *never*,' I mumbled despairingly.

'That sounds ungrammatical but heartfelt,' said Mr Speed, peering at me. 'Explain yourself, lad.'

'It was Holly all the time, Mr Speed. You got it all wrong.'

'I got it all wrong, did I?' said Mr Speed.

I wondered if I was in for another lecture, but he was shaking his head. 'Sorry, lad. I obviously jumped to the wrong conclusions. The old bionic glasses went all smeary on me. I'd better not try to play Cupid again.'

But he *did*!

After we'd trailed all round the museum we went into a special room where a lady got out this big

trunk of Victorian clothes and we all had to dress up and look daft. Mr Speed put on a top hat and a funny false moustache and then unearthed a pair of button boots from the bottom of the trunk.

'I know a lad who's into fancy footwear,'

he said. 'Here, Greg, put them on.'

They were nearly the right size but I couldn't get them buttoned up at all. They were far too fiddly.

'You need a buttonhook,' said the museum lady, producing this weird metal pointy thing with a bone handle.

'Aha! Let's pop this mob cap and pinny on you, Holly. You can be young Master Gregory's nursery maid,' said Mr Speed. 'Button the lad into his boots then, girl.'

'Certainly, Mr Speed,' said Holly. She seized the buttonhook as if it was a surgical instrument.

I didn't like the look of her grin at all now!

'Keep still, now,' she said, and she went *prod, prod, prod*. And *I* went 'Ow! Ow! Ow!'

'Don't be a silly baby, Master Gregory,' said Holly.

'OW! Cut it out, Holly! You're prodding right into my *leg*,' I protested.

'Good,' said Holly, under her breath. 'Why did you go and sit next to that stupid Samantha?'

'I didn't want to! It was all Mr Speed's fault. He made me. You know what he's like.'

'I know what *you're* like,' said Holly.

I swallowed. I took a very deep breath. I went all red and shuddery and yuckety-yuckety-yucky.

'But do you know *who* I like?' I said.

Holly looked at me, twiddling the buttonhook.

Then she grinned. I grinned back.

Guess who I got to sit next to on the coach going home!

And guess who is now my girlfriend!

Holly!

CLAIRE'S WORRY

Type in your worry:

I have this nightmare. It's really, really scary. I don't know what to do. I dream it every single night. Does anyone else have nightmares or am I the only one?

I've had bad dreams before. I've dreamt I've been walking to school and suddenly I'm just wearing my knickers and everyone starts staring and pointing and giggling. I always feel silly going to school the next day, as if it had really happened!

I've also had a falling dream. I'm at the top of this very long escalator and I suddenly trip and I go tumbling down and down and down . . . until I wake up with a start.

Then there's that dream when I'm having a huge row with my sister Judy in our bedroom. She's bigger and bossier than me but I bash her with my pillow and she falls flat on her bed. She doesn't move. I think she's just pretending she's hurt to scare me but my pillow feels strangely heavy and when I look inside I find it's full of rocks.

These are all pretty horrible dreams but they're not *too* bad. I don't think about them all the time. I can make sure they don't really happen. I can check I'm wearing my school uniform, avoid all escalators, and stop bashing Judy with my pillow. Well, I *do* still have pillow fights with her but they're mostly in fun. I have a quick pummel of the pillow first to make sure it's totally rock-free.

But now I'm having this new nightmare. I dream it every night. It's awful.

I've tried getting into Judy's bed. She moaned and fussed and said I was squashing her. It didn't work anyway. I still had the nightmare. I woke up screaming. Judy woke up too.

'What are you playing at, Claire? You woke me up! Hey, are you crying?'

'No,' I sobbed.

'Yes, you are,' said Judy. She suddenly put her arms round me. 'Shall I get Mum?'

'*No!*'

This is the trouble. I can't tell Mum or Dad. They will say it's all my own fault. And I suppose it is.

You see I secretly watched this ultra-scary video. Mum and Dad are quite strict about what films we're allowed to see. Especially me. I don't know what's the matter with me. I've always been so stupid. When I was a really little kid I sometimes got scared watching *cartoons*! There's a bit where horses gallop wildly in *Beauty and the Beast* that made me have bad dreams. I used to wake up crying that the horses were after me. My big brother Michael used to neigh and make galloping noises just to get me going.

Mum got fed up getting up to go to me in the night so ever since she's been very picky over what I'm allowed to watch. I kept telling her and telling her that I wasn't a silly baby any more. I was furious when she let Michael and Judy watch *Titanic* but she wouldn't let *me*.

'Of course you can't watch it, Claire. You'd dream you were drowning and then you'd wet the bed,' Michael chortled.

I hated being left out. I knew silly old movies couldn't scare me any more. Or so I thought.

But then I watched *The Monster*. I wonder if you've seen it? It's been a *big* talking point at our school. Heaps of kids go on about how great it is and say it's the scariest film ever, ever, ever. Some kids say it didn't scare *them* one bit. I think they're fibbing. I bet they haven't seen so much as the trailer.

I got to see it on Saturday. Mum and Judy had gone up to London because she had a music exam and then they were going shoe shopping afterwards. I was supposed to go too but I made a fuss. I *hate* listening while Judy plays her violin. She sounds like chalk squeaking on a blackboard. I have to put my fingers in my ears and then Judy says I'm putting her off deliberately. And shoe shopping is *soooo* boring, unless

58

you're looking for something cool like football boots or trainers.

So I stayed at home with Dad and Michael. Michael had his friend, Luke, round. They usually go into Michael's room and try to access rude things on the Internet, *I* know. But Dad was outside washing and polishing the car which takes him for ever, so Luke casually produced the video of *The Monster* from his backpack.

'Fancy watching a bit, Mike?'

'Wow!' said Michael, eyes goggling. 'You bet!'

'I'm watching too,' I said.

'There's no way *you're* watching, baby,' said Michael. He tried to push me out the living room while Luke slotted the video into the machine.

'There's *every* way I'm watching it – or I'll tell Dad,' I said.

I don't *like* being a telltale but when you have bossy big brothers and sisters you have to use any means at your disposal to get your own way.

So I won. I watched *The Monster*. Well, nearly half of it. Then we heard Dad coming back inside the house so we switched over to a sports programme, sharpish.

You have no idea how appalling *The Monster* is.

Far, far, far, *far* worse than you can ever imagine. I kept on telling myself it was just a silly old film. It wasn't a *real* monster. But it looked so real when it rose up out of the river, sickly green, oozing slime, and semi-transparent so you could see all its horrible heart and liver and lungs and long long coils of intestines, some of them hanging *out* and spurting terrible sludgy streams of poo.

Luke whooped with laughter, but it was very high-pitched. Michael started biting his nails. The

Monster started oozing up out of sinks and baths and even *toilets*. It devoured everything – dogs, cats, babies in buggies, screaming schoolchildren, frantic mothers, fighting fathers. The Monster even swallowed this huge fat man and you *saw* him being digested inside it, getting covered in bile, bits disintegrating before your very eyes.

Luke stopped laughing. Michael nearly bit his fingers right off. I stared at the screen helplessly, unable to move. The Monster seemed to ooze right out of the television set into my head. It was there, pulsing inside my brain, ready to ooze its way into my dreams.

They are the worst nightmares ever. I don't know what I'm going to do. I start feeling vaguely sick at teatime. I go out in the garden and play afterwards but all the time I'm kicking a football about or running up and down with my skipping rope I'm thinking about the Monster. When I'm watching television It's there too, slithering into Central Perk and nibbling Phoebe and Rachel and Monica like sweets.

Then Mum starts nagging that it's time for bed and the Monster is lurking on the stairs, in the bathroom, under my bed. Dad comes to read to Judy and me but the Monster paces the corridors of Hogwarts too, munching Harry Potter into mincemeat.

After Dad tucks us up and puts the light out I whisper to Judy, desperate to keep her awake. I talk about all the boy bands she's currently nuts on and the new boots she wants in Bertie's and the boy on the bike who waves to her every morning and whether this means he really fancies her. This is all terminally boring, boring, boring but it means Judy will keep chatting to me. But no matter how I try to keep the conversation going eventually she starts mumbling nonsense and then she sighs and gives a little snore. She is asleep, dreaming about boys and bands and bikes and boots.

I struggle to stay awake because I know what *I'm* going to dream about. I hear Michael go to bed. Sometimes I even hear Mum and Dad go to bed. I play the silliest games to stop myself sleeping. I go through all my favourites.

 Hero: David Beckham.
Friend: Holly, and Lisa's OK too.

 Hobby: football.
Teacher: Mr Speed.
Colour: anything

but slime green.

But no matter which rainbow hue I choose this sickening slime green oozes over it and I'm dreaming the Monster is coming to get me. I dream it every single night.

I waited to see if anyone typed in anything helpful on the Worry Website. There were *heaps* of comments. Everyone said they had nightmares too. I counted. There were thirty. That meant every single person in the class. No, wait a minute. *I* didn't comment on my own worry.

Mr Speed saw me scrolling down the screen, re-counting.

'I'm glad to see you practising your maths as well as your IT skills, Claire.'

'Thirty! It *is*. Someone's messing about, commenting twice,' I said.

'Not necessarily,' said Mr Speed. 'Not if we count the entire class, pupils and teacher.'

'Did *you* put a comment, Mr Speed?'

'Now, you know perfectly well all contributions to the Worry Website are strictly confidential,' said Mr Speed.

I read them with great interest, trying to work out which was his.

I dream I've lost my old teddy Cuddle and I search everywhere and once I woke up and I still couldn't find him because he'd fallen out of bed and I cried.

I imagine Mr Speed crying for his teddy. Perhaps not.

I have awful nightmares too. Last night I dreamt about my mum and it should have been

lovely but she turned into a wicked witch and cast a spell on me so I couldn't talk.

I don't know if Mr Speed has still got a mum but I can't *ever* imagine him not talking, even in his dreams.

My biggest nightmare is dreaming that I'm with my dad and it's all happy, happy, happy at first but then he starts getting cross with me and my little brother and my mum so he storms off and I wait and I wait but he doesn't come back.

That's quite definitely Samantha. So what did Mr Speed put?

Aha!

I have this terrible nightmare that my feet develop throbbing bunions overnight and so I have to give up my brilliant career as a Premier-League footballer and retrain as a TEACHER!!!

I looked Mr Speed up and down.

'That's *your* nightmare, isn't it, Mr Speed?'

'The Worry Website insists on anonymity,' said Mr Speed.

'Yeah, but I *know* it's you! You weren't *really* a Premier-League footballer, were you?'

Mr Speed crumpled a piece of paper into a ball.

'Haven't you read about Speedy of United in all your football annuals?'

He dropped the paper ball and then aimed a nifty kick at it. Only it wasn't nifty. It wasn't even a kick. He missed it altogether.

I shook my head.

'You should have seen me *before* my bunions,' he said. 'So, Claire, we'll do a swapsie. You know my worst nightmare. Tell me yours.'

'Oh, it's – it's stupid,' I mumbled.

'But scary?'

'Very, very scary.'

Mr Speed looked at me carefully.

'You look like a little panda. Dark circles under the eyes. Are these nightmares so bad they stop you sleeping?'

'I don't *dare* sleep.'

Mr Speed raised his eyebrows.

'So tell me all about this nightmare. You can remember it?'

'I can't ever forget it,' I said. 'It's about this monster made out of green slime and—'

'Say no more!' said Mr Speed. 'I got the video out last week. Yep. It's seriously scary. Do Mum and Dad know you've watched it?'

'No!'

'Ah. I *see!*'

'You won't tell, will you, Mr Speed?'

'Let's see if we can radically edit your nightmare. Then we won't have to tell.'

'What do you mean? You can't edit nightmares. It just happens. And it's horrible.'

'I know it's horrible, Claire. But maybe you can control it, change it around a little bit. You've made it up inside your head, haven't you? It's like a story you've written in your sleep. OK, let's look on it as a first draft. Now you need to rewrite it. Change the scenario. You've got to get the better of this monster.'

'You mean flick my fingers and go zap and the Monster dies?' I said sarcastically. 'I don't think it would work.'

'No, probably not. It sounds a bit too powerful to be zapped into oblivion just like that. But you can be powerful too, Claire. What are your strengths, eh?'

I frowned at him.

'I'm good at football. But that's no use, not when it comes to the Monster.'

'Maybe it is. Kick a football at him. Aim right where it hurts. Make him double up.'

'Mr Speed, in the film the Monster defeats a whole *army*.'

'But this is the Monster in your head. He defeats whole armies, yes – but he's *very* wary of small girls with footballs.'

I thought Mr Speed was just being silly to cheer me up. He *did* make me feel a bit better when I was at school. But when I went home I started worrying again.

I got into bed with Judy and hung onto her tightly.

I tried very, very, very hard to stay awake – but eventually the duvet started turning slime green and I was dreaming and the Monster was there, oozing all over me.

I screamed and ran. The Monster was right behind me, reaching out, ready to slide his glistening tentacles round my neck. I tried running faster, speeding along. That made me think of Mr Speed. I looked down and there was a football at my feet. I was kicking it as I ran. I nudged it up into the air, caught hold of it, turned, and threw it right at the Monster's middle.

The ball got bigger. The Monster got smaller. Much, much smaller. It doubled up, wailing. It rocked itself, oozing lots of slime.

'There! That's shown you, you horrible Monster. Don't you dare come worrying me any more!'

The Monster groaned. It was shrinking rapidly now. It limped away, whimpering.

I kicked my football high in the air and then caught it in triumph . . .

'Ow! My head! Get *off*, Claire,' Judy yelled.

'Oops! Sorry. I thought it was a football,' I said, giggling.

'Look, get back to your *own* bed.'

'OK,' I said. I jumped out and climbed under my own duvet.

'You're all right, then?' Judy whispered. 'Look, come back with me if you get that nightmare again. Just don't bash me about the head again, OK?'

'I'm fine, Judy, really,' I said, yawning. 'Sh! Let's go to sleep now.'

I cuddled down under the duvet and slept properly. I didn't have the nightmare about the Monster. I had a funny dream about football. Mr Speed and I were on the same team. Mr Speed ran in a funny hobbly way because of his bunions but he managed to pass the ball to me – and I scored a brilliant goal.

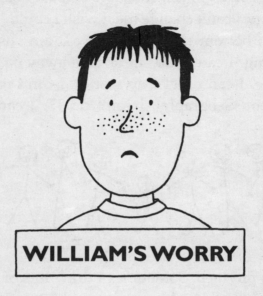

WILLIAM'S WORRY

Type in your worry:

I am useless at everything.

That's it. And it is dead depressing to be me. I am William. I can't always spell it properly when I write in pencil. But it's OK on the computer because it does a wiggly red line under the word if you've spelt it wrong. Almost every word I tap out ends up with wiggly red lines.

I feel as if *I* am all wrong and there is a wiggly red line under me. You can change

69

your spelling (though sometimes I have to try for *ages* and I have to ask someone helpful like Holly or Claire) but I can't change me. I wish I could.

I am bottom in the class. I am useless at everything. I can't add up or take away or multiply or divide. I can't make up stories. I can't remember History or Geography. I can't do IT. I can't draw.

I just do pin men. Sometimes I draw lots of pin men and they are all laughing at a stupid little pin boy.

My mum and dad don't laugh at me. My mum cries and my dad shouts. My brother says I am thick. He is younger than me but he's clever. His name is Richard. Sometimes Dad calls him Dick. He is definitely a Clever Dick.

Dad sometimes shortens my name too. He calls me Willie. They call me that at school sometimes too. It is *awful* having a name that sounds rude and makes people giggle.

Mr Speed called me Wee Willie Winkie today. I nearly cried.

'It's just a nursery rhyme, William,' said Mr Speed. 'Oh, don't look so stricken, lad. Here. You call *me* a silly name.'

I blinked at him.

'Go on, be a devil. Think up something really silly.'

I swallowed. 'Mr Silly Speed?' I said.

Mr Speed sighed. 'You're not over-endowed with imagination, are you, lad?'

I hung my head.

'Cheer up!' said Mr Speed. He ruffled my hair. 'There!' He wiped his fingers on my fringe. 'That's better. My fingers were very sticky.'

I felt my hair worriedly.

'I'm *joking*, William,' said Mr Speed.

The bell went for lunch. My tummy gave a loud rumble.

'If the bell electrics failed us, your stomach would act as a little alarm clock – *gurgle, gurgle* whenever it's lunchtime. What greater use is that?' said Mr Speed. 'I like a boy with a healthy appetite.'

I wasn't sure if he was joking or not. He seemed to

change his mind on dinner duty. It was fish fingers and baked beans and chips, and if you finish first you get seconds. So I went gobble, gobble and stood up quick, ready to dash back to the serving hatch.

'My goodness, William, take it easy!' said Mr Speed. 'Sit down and *chew*. You've got your entire plateful stuffed in your mouth! You'll choke to death, lad.'

'But – I – want – seconds – Mr – Speed!'

'William! Close your mouth! Good lord, lad, you're spraying half-masticated morsels all over us. Watch out, Samantha. We'll have to issue you with protective clothing if William carries on chomping with such abandon.'

I had to wait and chew until my mouth was empty. It wasn't *fair*. Half the other boys got to the hatch before me. Greg got the last portion of extra chips.

I looked at Mr Speed.

'Don't look so reproachful, lad, I can't stand it. OK, OK. My concerns for your digestion have done you out of a few chips—'

'A whole plateful, Mr Speed!'

'I haven't had *my* lunch yet. Stay behind and I dare say I'll donate a chip or two to you.'

He gave me *all* his chips – yummy, yummy, yummy!

'Slow down! You don't have to cram them all in together, William. I marvel at the capacity of that mouth of yours. Now, how are things at home, lad?'

I shrugged. I wouldn't have known what to say even if my mouth *wasn't* full of chips. I mean, home's *home*. What is there to say about it?

'Mum and Dad OK?'

'Mmm,' I said, swallowing.

'And how are you getting on with your brother?'

I didn't say anything but I must have pulled a face.

'That bad, eh?' said Mr Speed, laughing.

He lowered his voice. 'What about the little bed-wetting problem?'

I looked round nervously. Mr Speed had stopped everyone calling me Wetty Willie but I didn't want them *reminded*.

'It's heaps better, Mr Speed. Mum took me to the doctor, like you said, and I got this medicine.'

'Great! So things are looking up, William?'

'I suppose.'

'But you still feel a bit . . . useless?'

I stared at him. Mr Speed is magic. I wondered

how on earth he knew. He could have read it on the Worry Website but you're not allowed to sign your name so he couldn't possibly work out it was *me*.

'You're not useless, William.'

'I *am*, Mr Speed.'

'No, no, no, William.'

'Yes, yes, yes, Mr Speed. I can't do *nothing*.'

'Anything. And you *can*.' Mr Speed screwed up his face. 'You're very good at . . .'

I waited.

'You're a very good boy, full stop,' said Mr Speed.

'But I wish I could be good *at* something, Mr Speed,' I said.

'Well, perhaps we can give you a bit of extra help with your school work?'

I must have pulled another face.

'Don't look so appalled! OK, OK, we'll try another tack. What about games? We could maybe get Claire to help you with your footie skills.'

'I'm useless at football, Mr Speed. I always trip myself up when I try to kick the ball.'

'Look, lad, we're not trying to turn you into David Beckham.'

'I had a David Beckham haircut in the holidays. My dad said it would make me look tough. But it didn't work.'

'Never you mind, William,' said Mr Speed. 'We'll

make *something* work for you, just you wait and see. Things are going to start looking up for you, lad.'

So I waited. Nothing much happened in the afternoon. I came bottom in the spelling test. I painted a snail picture all different colours in Art. I used too much water and the blue ran into the yellow and  the red dribbled all down the page so that it looked as if my snail had had a nasty accident.

My mum got mad at me for getting paint all over my school trousers. Richard and I got into a fight  over which of us owned a blue biro. I *know* it was my biro. But Richard won. So I couldn't do my homework as I didn't have anything to write with. Then Dad came home and Richard and I played catch with him in the garden. Well, Dad and Richard played catch. I played drop.

Then we had spag bol for tea (I'm not even going to *try* to spell it all out). It was hotter than I thought so I had to spit my first mouthful out. Mum thumped me and Dad shouted at me for crying and Richard laughed at me for being a baby.

I went to bed. And don't tell anyone but I wet myself because I forgot to take my special medicine.

Things haven't looked up *yet*.

When I got to school I looked at the Worry Website to see if I'd got any comments.

I'm sure you're not useless at everything.

Don't worry, I'm pretty useless at everything too.

I bet you're useFUL, not useLESS.

Things started to look up quite a bit. I felt so pleased that people didn't seem to think I was useless after all. Though of course they didn't know it was me. Perhaps if I'd put my name they'd have said I was ultra-ultra-ultra-useless. Especially as I can't always spell my name right.

We had another spelling test which was a bit of a nasty surprise as we only usually have one a week.

'Don't look so down-hearted, children. There are going to be two special prizes to spur you on. Two of my very special pens, no less.'

Mr Speed produced a pen from each pocket like a cowboy whipping out two guns. Mr Speed's pens *are* special. They are black and they write with a very fine line. They make the worst handwriting in the world look much neater. Mr Speed goes crazy if any of us borrow his special pens. But now he was giving away *two* as prizes – and it wasn't even the end of term.

I wished I was good at spelling. But I am such rubbish at spelling I knew it was absolutely no use hoping to win a pen.

'I want you all to try very hard,' said Mr Speed, and then he started saying all these words.

There was a lot of sighing and muttering and nibbling of pens. Some of the class whispered.

'I want absolutely *no* conferring,' said Mr Speed.

Nobody tried to confer with me anyway. Which is not surprising. I can't even *spell* surprising.

Mr Speed told us to have a go at spelling everything, so I did. Even the very, very hard words. I'm not going to write them here – I'll never get them right.

I did lots and lots of crossings out. So many that my paper tore. But it didn't really matter. I knew I wasn't going to do well in the spelling test. I knew I was going to do really, really badly.

I was right. We had to swap papers. Lisa marked mine and I marked hers. Lisa is clever. She got fourteen out of twenty. She is also kind. I didn't get *any* of my spellings right. She put up her hand to talk to Mr Speed.

'William's very nearly spelt "naughty" right, Mr Speed. And his "because" has only got one mistake. So could he have a half each for those?'

'Absolutely not,' said Mr Speed. 'A word is either spelt correctly or it isn't. And William's *isn't*.'

'But that's not very fair, Mr Speed,' said Lisa.

'Life isn't fair, Lisa,' said Mr Speed gently.

I hoped Lisa might win one of Mr Speed's pens but Holly got *eighteen* spellings completely correct. She was dead chuffed to win the pen, especially as her little sister Hannah had leant too hard on Holly's old pen and made it go all splodgy.

'Maybe you'll win the second pen, Lisa,' I said hopefully.

But Samantha got sixteen spellings absolutely ace-standard correct. She batted her big blue eyes, looking very, very hopeful.

'Now we have the *second* prize-winner,' said Mr Speed. Strangely, he wasn't looking at Samantha. He was looking at *me*!

'This goes to the child who has had the sheer

dogged temerity to resist all my persuasive teaching skills and persists in being a truly inventively gargantuan appalling speller.'

I gaped at Mr Speed. I hadn't understood a word he was saying. But I understood the *next* bit.

'The second pen is awarded to the child who has the *most* spelling mistakes. Step forward, William!'

So *I* got the second prize pen. Some of the children groaned and said it wasn't fair – but most of them clapped. Greg even *cheered*!

I felt very, very, very pleased.

I didn't feel exactly *proud* though. I am a bit thick but I'm not completely stupid. I knew it was just a booby prize. It's not the same getting a prize for being the worst at something. I still wished I could be the *best* at something so I wouldn't feel quite so useless.

Mr Speed always makes up a story for us after spelling. He uses every single spelling word within the story. It was one of his *When I was a little boy* stories. He told us his accommodation was a miniature but pleasant house and his parents paid him every attention even though it was occasionally necessary to discipline him because he was so naughty. He enjoyed eating delicious breakfasts, especially sausages. He ate his substantial sausages with such determined commitment that he invariably made himself physically sick but this was a penalty he bore with relative indifference. His sausage consumption was brilliant training for the daily Enormous Mouthful contest that took place at lunchtime.

Mr Speed wanted to stop his story then and there because he'd used up all the hard spelling words but we all complained and said, 'No, Mr Speed, go on, tell us more,' because we all wanted to hear about the Enormous Mouthful contest.

'You mean I've never told you about the Enormous Mouthful contest?' said Mr Speed, looking astonished. 'Well, maybe it's just as well. If I tell you about it you'll only start up something similar yourselves.'

'No we won't, Mr Speed,' we all chorused.

'Oh yes you will!'

'Oh no we won't!'

We went on like this, getting louder, Mr Speed conducting us with his arms. Then he quickly put his finger to his lips and we all *whispered* – even me. This is a game we play when Mr Speed is in a good mood.

Then he told us all about the food they had for school dinners when he was a little boy. You couldn't choose in those long ago days. You never ever had chips (my favourites). You had disgusting things like smelly stew all glistening with fat and grey mince that looked as if someone had chewed it all up. You had cabbage like old seaweed and lumpy mashed potato and tinned peas that smelt like feet.

'But we ate it all up because if you didn't you weren't allowed to have pudding. Puddings were the whole *point* of school dinners. We had jam roly-poly and bread-and-butter pudding and chocolate sponge with chocolate sauce and apple pie and custard and absolute best of all, trifle. There were also a lot of boring puddings like rice and semolina and something particularly revolting called tapioca that looked like frog spawn – but even these were palatable because we were given spoonfuls of jam or brown sugar or raisins. Those of us who were particularly greedy wangled *two* spoonfuls. These were to be savoured. However, the milk puddings needed to be golloped down as quickly as possible because they were so horrible. *That* was the start of the Enormous Mouthful club. Someone got hold of a big serving spoon and we had this ridiculous contest to see who could swallow the largest mouthful.'

'Did you win, Mr Speed?'

'Do you think I would have been such a rude and ill-mannered and mischievous child as to take part in such an indigestion-inducing eating contest?' said Mr Speed.

'YES!' we yelled.

Mr Speed grinned and bowed. 'You know me well, my children. Yes, I took part. Yes, I choked and spluttered and snorted and got violent hiccups. And *yes*, I won the Enormous Mouthful contest.' Mr Speed paused. 'But you children are strictly forbidden to take part in any similar contest. Do you all hear me?'

'Yes, Mr Speed,' we said.

'And to hear . . . ?'

'Is to obey,' we chorused.

We heard all right. But of course we didn't obey. We had our very own Enormous Mouthful contest at lunchtime. It was not quite as easy for us. We didn't have milk puddings which are

soft and slippy. We have bulky, crunchy, crispy food that won't go with one swallow. We had to experiment and do an awful lot of chewing (and a little choking too).

Chips proved to be the easiest food for the Enormous Mouthful contest. My favourite.

I shovelled up an entire plateful of chips and crammed them all into my mouth and I WON the Enormous Mouthful contest!

I came FIRST.

So I'm not useless. I'm the champion Enormous Mouthful Eater of all time. Whoopee! Whoopee! Whoopee!

Mr Speed was right. Things have looked up *enormously*.

SAMANTHA'S WORRY

Type in your worry:

I miss my dad. It's just not the same now he's gone. And my mum is either sad or snappy nowadays. And my little brother is ever so naughty and keeps spoiling all my things. And no-one wants to be my boyfriend. And I don't think my teacher likes me any more either. He always used to pick me to be his special messenger but now he picks Holly. Or Greg. Or Claire. Or even William.

It's so awful. I've always been the girl everyone *likes*. Everyone always wants to sit next to me or be my partner. Everyone wants to be invited for tea at my house or come to my party.

But now it's all changed.

Dad went last year. He and Mum had lots of rows but everyone's parents have rows. I didn't *like* it but it didn't really bother me. My little brother Simon used to crawl into my bed and sit on my lap and he made me cup my hands over his funny little sticky-out ears so he couldn't hear the shouting.

I didn't have anyone to put their hands over my ears but I didn't mind too much. I wanted to know what was going on. I was always on Dad's side no matter what. I love my mum but she's not *Dad*. Dad looks like a film star, he really does, with lovely blond hair and deep blue eyes and he's really fit too because he works out and plays a lot of sport. That was what Mum and Dad rowed about. Dad always flirted with all the ladies he met at badminton and tennis and swimming. My mum used to go too but then she had me and couldn't get out so much and then she had Simon and stayed a bit plump so she didn't want to wear tight sporty clothes anyway.

Dad took me sometimes. He got me my own special little tennis racket and threw the ball at me again and again. We went swimming on Sunday mornings and he showed me how to dive and swim right down to the bottom of the deep end and he called me his little dolphin.

But then he met this horrible woman, Sandy, at his gym and Mum found out. Dad didn't stop seeing Sandy. He packed his bag and walked out and stopped seeing *us*.

He said he wasn't leaving me, he was just leaving Mum. He said he was still my dad and he loved me lots and lots and lots and he'd see me every single week. But that hasn't worked out because he and Sandy have moved away and now that Sandy's going to have a baby, Dad doesn't come over so much. I haven't seen him for weeks now. He was supposed to come last weekend for Simon's birthday, he absolutely *promised*, but the day before he rang to say Sandy had got these special tickets for a trip to Paris as a surprise so they were going there instead.

Mum shouted down the phone that he obviously

couldn't care less about his own son and his birthday. Dad said that he loved Simon very much but perhaps it wasn't good for him to see him so often anyway because Simon got very over-excited and silly and the visits were obviously upsetting him.

Simon kicked Sandy hard on the shin the last time we went round to Dad's new place.

I wished I was young enough to kick Sandy too.

Mum said we didn't *need* Dad at Simon's party, we'd have a much better time by ourselves. But we didn't.

I don't suppose Dad will come to my party now either. No-one will come to my party. No-one likes me any more. It was so awful on the bus when we all went to the museum. Greg was horrible to me. I thought he really *liked* me. But he's nuts on Holly instead. Holly hates me too. She always pulls a face and sighs when I start talking. And Mr Speed likes Holly best now, I just know he does. He's always chatting to her. He makes a great big fuss of Claire too. And though he's always telling Greg off you can tell he thinks he's really funny. Mr Speed even likes silly-willy William more than me.

William banged right into me at lunchtime and spilt his orange squash all down my school blouse. I shouted at him. William looked upset in his silly, goofy way.

'I'm sorry, Samantha. I didn't *mean* to. I was just in a hurry to get seconds.'

'Look at my blouse! It's all *orange*,' I said, plucking at my dripping blouse.

'It looks like a pretty pattern. Orange is a lovely colour,' said William. 'Here, let's dry it a bit.'

He picked up the messy old cloth we use to wipe the tables and started dabbing at me, smearing bits of old chip and pizza sauce all over my blouse, making it a hundred times worse.

'Leave *off*, William. Don't be so *stupid*,' I shouted.

William burst into tears like a baby. Mr Speed came dashing up.

'Hey hey hey! Why are two of my favourite pupils

abusing each other so bitterly?' he asked. 'Don't *cry*, William.'

'I'm not *anyone's* favourite,' I said, and I burst into tears too.

Mr Speed tutted and sighed and mopped us both. He told William he could have extra chips if he stopped crying. William cheered up immediately and went bounding off.

'I think your problems are possibly less easily solved, Samantha,' said Mr Speed. 'But you'll certainly feel a *little* better if we find you a change of blouse. That one's sopping. How about changing into your PE shirt?'

'I took it home for Mum to wash,' I sniffed.

'Oh dear, oh dear. Never mind. Come with me.'

I trailed after him miserably.

'I might have someone's spare PE top in the classroom cupboard,' said Mr Speed.

While he was searching high and low amongst ancient confiscated Pokémon cards and single plimsolls and dried-up felt tips I went and looked to see if I had any replies on the Worry Website.

Comments:

My dad is so scary I wish he WASN'T at home with us.

My dad's great but he's always tired because of his new

job so I hardly ever get to talk to him either.

My mum gets cross too. AND my dad.

Yeah, and MY little sister can be a right pain too, and as a matter of fact I don't see my mum but I don't go on and on about it. And I can't help it if Mr Speed sometimes picks me to do stuff now. It doesn't mean he's stopped liking you.

Mr Speed came and peered over my shoulder.

'Budge over, Samantha.'

He typed:

Of course your teacher likes you. He is a wonderful, kindly man who likes everyone. ESPECIALLY sad little souls going through a bad patch.

'There!' said Mr Speed. 'Do you think this particular sad little soul will be comforted, Samantha?'

'Maybe just a little bit,' I said.

'It's probably surprising to an extremely popular girl like you that someone can feel so lonely,' said Mr Speed.

'Mmm!' I said.

'I can't find a spare shirt anywhere. Come with me. We'll see if Mrs Holmes has a hidden cache in her office.'

We went down the corridor to the main entrance. Mr Speed bobbed into the Secretary's office while I hung around, picking at my sticky sodden blouse. There were paintings stuck all over the walls. Some of them had been there a while and were curling at the edges. There were a few *My Family* paintings our class did last year.

My picture was there. I'd painted my dad and my mum and my little brother and me, all of us standing in a line and smiling. The red paint had run a bit when I did my face, so my lips were huge.

I stared at my stupid gigantic grin and then I punched the paper, bashing my own pinkly-painted face. My little brother was grinning too. It was his fault Dad didn't come any more, because he behaved so badly. I hit my little brother too. The paper tore a little, so that my mum's head was nearly split in two. I didn't care. If she hadn't shouted so much Dad might have stayed.

I looked at Dad. I'd painted him extra carefully, though I couldn't get the colours quite right. His hair was bright lemon, his eyes ultramarine, his cheeks scarlet. I wasn't really that great at painting. I couldn't make my dad look handsome enough.

I'd printed MY FAMILY underneath. But Dad wasn't really part of our family any more. He was part of a brand-new family with Sandy. He was going to have this new baby too. I hoped it wouldn't be a little girl. He'd love her much more than he loved me.

My fist clenched and I punched Dad hard, again and again, harder and harder.

'Hey, hey! Stop it! Samantha, you'll hurt your poor hand,' Mr Speed shouted, rushing out of Mrs Holmes's office.

'I don't care,' I yelled. I punched my painting again, even though there were beads of blood on my knuckles and my arm throbbed all the way up past my elbow.

'Well, *I* care,' said Mr Speed. 'Good lord, child, *stop* it.'

He caught hold of my hand. I burst into tears. Mr Speed patted me gently on the back and then led me into Mrs Holmes's office. She found me a box of tissues, a clean blouse and a big bandage for my fist.

Mr Speed came back to collect me. 'Ah! All mopped up?'

I nodded.

'I'll take you back to the classroom, sweetheart.

Dear, oh dear. I'd better have a word with your mum when she comes to collect you.'

'I don't want you to have a word with my mum, Mr Speed. I want you to have a word with my *dad*.' I looked up at him. 'You're great at fixing things, aren't you? I bet you could sort out all the worries on our website. Well, why can't you sort out mine? Can't you make my dad come back?'

Mr Speed sighed.

'I can't do that, Samantha. I can sometimes solve little tiny problems but I can't do a thing about big sad problems. Not even mine. My own marriage broke up a while ago. I know just how you're feeling, poppet.'

'Did you leave your children, Mr Speed?'

'I don't have any children,' he said. He gave a funny little grin. 'Maybe teaching all you lot put me off having any of my own?'

'But if you *did* have children would you walk out on them?'

'Oh, Samantha, how can I possibly answer that one?' said Mr Speed.

'I bet you wouldn't,' I said. I thought about my dad. I saw him walking off, his arm round Sandy. I stood still in the corridor. 'I hate my dad,' I whispered. The words tasted bad in my mouth so I spat them out louder. '*I hate my dad!*'

'Yes. I can understand that,' said Mr Speed. 'Though you still love him lots too. But you're very, very angry with him. That's why you started punching his picture. But that's not really a good idea, is it? You only hurt your poor old hand.' He carefully patted my bandage.

'What do you think I should do then, Mr Speed? Punch my *dad*?'

'That's maybe not a good idea either.'

'Our Simon kicked his girlfriend. She got a big bruise on her leg.'

'Oh dear. I shall wear shinpads when your Simon comes up into the Juniors. He's in Miss Morgan's class, isn't he? She'll channel all his energy into finger painting or digging in the sandpit. Excellent activities! How about a spot of digging, Samantha? How about getting a spade and having a good dig in your garden whenever you feel especially cross or miserable?'

'We live in a flat, Mr Speed. We haven't even got a window box.'

'Ah. Well . . . perhaps we could purloin a little patch of the school garden?' Mr Speed smiled. 'Let's go and have a look round, see if we can find the right little corner.'

So Mr Speed and I went across the playground

over to the garden. I'd played on the grass heaps of times but I'd never really looked properly at the garden bit before. I peered at the plants. Mr Speed started spouting all these long Latin names. I listened politely, not really taking any of it in until Mr Speed pointed to a patch of earth behind a big bush.

'Aha! This looks the perfect plot. OK, Samantha. This is your patch. I'll find you a spade. You can dig here any playtime or lunchtime, before school, after school, whenever.'

I tried having a little dig there and then. I couldn't do too much because of my sore hand. I wasn't very good at it at first. I was too quick and clumsy and couldn't budge the hard earth. Mr Speed showed me how to do it slowly and rhythmically, putting my foot on the spade, straightening up so I wouldn't hurt my back.

'That's it! Ah, you've got into the swing of things now. We'll be hiring you out on building sites at this rate. You'll have muscles like Madonna by the end of the month.'

I think digging *has* made me stronger. Greg was mucking

around in the corridor doing a silly dance and showing off in front of Holly. He did a twiddly bit and banged right into me. I pushed him away so hard he nearly fell over! That'll teach him. I can't stick Greg now. I don't envy Holly one bit. I wouldn't want him as a boyfriend if you paid me.

I don't want *William* as my boyfriend either. But he seems to think he is!

I cheered up a bit after I had my first little dig. I felt mean for making William cry so I went up to him after school. He cowered away as if I was going to hit him. That made me feel worse – so I put my arm round him.

'Sorry I yelled at you, William,' I said, and I gave him a hug.

I thought that was it. It *was* as far as I was concerned. But now William goes pink whenever I go near him and he follows me around like a little dog. He tries to carry my schoolbag and rushes to get my school lunch for me and whenever I go for a dig William trails after me and wants to dig too.

I had a little moan about it to Mr Speed.

'It was *my* private patch, Mr Speed, and now William wants to dig too.'

'Yeah, I can see it's annoying having young William under your feet all the time, Samantha. But on the other hand he needs a bit of digging therapy himself.'

'OK, Mr Speed. But I wish he didn't have to dig on *my* bit. I tried planting an apple core just to see if it might just grow up into an apple tree and William dug it up the very next day.'

'Perhaps you could mark off your special bit and make sure William keeps to his? And I'll let you have a few seeds and bulbs if you fancy a spot of real gardening. That's a great idea.'

So I divided my patch into two and told William he could dig all he wanted on his own bit. Mr Speed brought us lots of lovely things to plant in our new gardens. Mine were a mixture of pretty flower seeds: pinks and pansies, primroses and sweet peas.

'And I'll see if I can get some raspberry canes too. They'll be a lot speedier than apple trees,' said Mr Speed. 'I thought you'd like to grow something to eat too, William, seeing as you're the lad of gargantuan appetite. I thought potatoes would be more in your line.

Think of all those chips! And we might go for something really exotic like a marrow. That *would* be a challenge for the Enormous Mouthful contest! But you'd better have a few flowers too.'

Mr Speed handed him a seed packet with a picture of deep purply-red-and-white little flowers on it. They were called Sweet Williams!

'I wish there was a flower called Sweet Samantha,' said Mr Speed.

So now I've stopped digging and started gardening. Little weeny green shoots are starting to grow through the very well-dug earth. They might just be little weeds though. We'll have to wait and see.

Mr Speed brought William and me a tomato plant today. My dad loves tomatoes. He can gollop up a whole pound, easy-peasy. If he comes to visit when my tomatoes are ripe I might offer him his very own home-grown tomato salad. But if he *doesn't* come then Mum and

Simon and me will eat them all up. Well, I'll save enough for a special tomato sandwich for Mr Speed.

I have one worry less. My teacher really *does* like me lots!

The first Worry Website story about Holly was made available on the Internet last year by BOL and the Guardian. I suggested we have a competition to see if any children wanted to make up their own story about a child in Mr Speed's class who has a worry to type onto the website. I was delighted that there were 15,000 entries. The shortlisted stories I personally judged were all of such a high standard that it was agonizing only being able to choose one. But that one story was so special that it simply had to be the winner. It's by Lauren Roberts, aged twelve.

I'd planned to make Lauren's the last story in the book but it ends so sadly that I decided to add one more story myself, just to try to end things on a happy note.

So here is Lauren's wonderful prize-winning Worry Website story.

Jacqueline Wilson

LISA'S WORRY

Type in your worry:

I . . .

I think . . .

Oh, this is useless. I could type in a thousand worries if I had to, but I can't find one un-stupid enough to put in. I do that. Make up words from somewhere. I make lots of things up, fantasy things, like creatures and magical people so I can disappear into my own world whenever I like.

I don't need to disappear anywhere at home though; I've got my mum. She's the best mum in the world.

Sometimes I draw her with flowing black hair and piercing blue eyes, trapped in a tower waiting for a prince to come and rescue her. My mum is beautiful, and she's trapped. Stuck in a flat with me and the wicked wizard who spends all our money on beer and cigarettes.

The wicked wizard is my dad. We only see him at teatime and in the morning now. He's out all night at the pub. My mum keeps saying that he'll change. He never will.

I remember when I was little, and we all used to sit on their big bed and he used to read to me. My favourite was *The Ugly Duckling*. I can remember my mum reading the swan's parts in a smooth soft voice, and Dad doing the ugly duckling and the ducks' parts in funny high-pitched voices that made me giggle. I loved that room. It had a nice musky smell. We had to move when I was seven because Dad got a new job. That's when he started changing.

He was always late home, and then he went straight

to bed. He stopped playing games with me and Mum. He didn't talk any more, only shouted.

I missed my old school and my best friend, Sarah. We used to be inseparable. The teachers would rush up to us before breaktimes and ask us to keep the Reception classes under control, because we were one-hundred-per-cent reliable. We kept them occupied by doing this little comedy routine. Their favourite was the 'she's behind you' routine. Sarah stood in front and said, 'I wonder where Lisa could be' – and just then I'd run past behind her and pull funny faces. The classes would all point and shout, 'She's behind you!' Then I'd hide again. They loved that.

When I came to my new school I didn't fit in. Some of the girls tried to talk to me but I wouldn't talk to them. I really wanted to make some friends but whenever someone talked to me I remembered Sarah and felt guilty.

The boys ignored me until we did football in PE (girls v boys) and we won 6–3. I scored five goals. Then all the boys picked me for their footie team, and reckoned I was dead sporty. They picked me for other teams, like rounders and basketball, but soon I realized I couldn't hit a rounders ball with a bat the size of Calcutta and I couldn't score a basket if they paid me.

Mrs Bryn shouted at me a lot for being behind in class and not doing homework. I was glad to move up to Mr Speed's class.

Mr Speed was great at cheering me up. He helped me catch up with my work and make friends. It felt great.

But one day after I'd been to Claire's house, I came home and my mum was crying. She said that she'd just banged her arm and bruised it. I hugged her tight and told her she'd be all right. She had hurt her face too, but it didn't cross my mind what might be going on until I went to bed. It was just as I fell asleep that I understood that my dad – the same squeaky duckling, imaginary games, laughing, smiling dad that I had loved with all my heart right up until the point he changed – could be hurting my mother.

I was afraid to leave my mum in the morning, so I started coughing like crazy, and she tucked me up on the sofa. I pretended to be asleep and heard my dad shouting and my mum trying not to let him wake me, which made him shout more.

I opened my eyes in time to see him hit Mum and leave. My body froze. As soon as the door closed I rushed to my mum's side.

The next day when he came back he was all lovey-

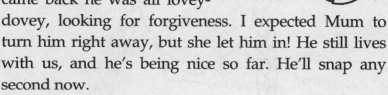

dovey, looking for forgiveness. I expected Mum to turn him right away, but she let him in! He still lives with us, and he's being nice so far. He'll snap any second now.

Type in your worry:

I'm starting to get spots.

After all, there are some things you don't want people to know.

NATASHA'S WORRY

Type in your worry:

I wish I could take part in the concert.

Mr Speed is organizing a concert. The whole class keeps going on about it. William is fussing because he can't do anything. Everyone else is singing or playing a musical instrument or reciting a poem or dancing. I can't sing or play or recite or dance. But people don't expect me to be able to perform. I can't even walk or talk. But it's OK. I manage. I use a wheelchair. It's electric and powerful so sometimes I can muck about chasing

the other kids. I have a special speaking machine too. My fingers work in a shaky sort of way so I can press the right button and words get said. Not always the words I *want*. I can't say *rude* words when I'm cross unless I spell them out laboriously. I usually choose to say short easy words because it's so much quicker.

It makes me sound a bit simple. I know I look it. But I'm NOT. I go to a special school but we have proper lessons, Maths and English and Science and stuff just like everyone else. And one day a week I go up the road and round the corner to Mapleton Juniors to see what it's like in an ordinary classroom.

Only it's not the slightest *bit* ordinary. They have this really wacky teacher Mr Speed. I wasn't sure I liked him at first. He leaps about a lot and shouts and uses weird long words. The teachers and helpers at my special school walk carefully and talk quietly and use words everyone can understand. I got a bit nervous when he came near me at first. My arms jerked about more than usual and I shrank down even smaller than usual. Most people think I'm younger than I am because I'm quite little. They treat you like a baby anyway if you use a wheelchair.

But not Mr Speed.

'Hello, Natasha,' he said, straight to me. Lots of people look at Wendy, my helper, even though they're talking to me.

I made my machine say hello back. Mr Speed told the class about my talking machine and asked if I'd say hello to them too. I did. Then I added, 'Let's make friends.' This was artful. I knew they'd all go, 'Aaah!' and say yes. You need to get children on your side. Sometimes they can be *sooo* mean. They can call you Spaz and Dummy and the Veggie. You can't have thin skin if you have a disability. Sometimes I've had to have skin like a *rhinoceros* to stop all the rude remarks hurting me.

But Mr Speed's class were all good to me right from the start. Almost *too* nice. The girls begged Wendy to let them push me around and they treated me like a doll, fussing with my hair and fiddling with my chair strap and speaking very loud and very s–l–o–w–l–y. The boys waved at me a bit nervously, keeping well clear of my wheelchair – in case I leapt up and bit them? They were all ever so polite though – apart from William. He didn't mean to be rude. He isn't that sort of kid. He just stared and stared and stared at me, as if I was an extraordinary television programme. The pretty girl, Samantha, gave him a little nudge and whispered to him not to stare so.

'Why?' said William.

'Because it's rude,' Samantha hissed.

'But she looks so *funny*,' said William.

'Sh!' said Samantha, going pink.

'She can't hear, can she?' said William. 'She can't *speak*.'

It seems to me that it's old William who has the disability – a *mental* one. But I suppose he can't help it. Same as I can't help looking funny. William's right about that. My mum says I've got a lovely smile and my dad says I'm his Pretty Princess and Wendy says I've got beautiful blue eyes – but they are simply being kind. Mr Speed says I have lovely long hair. He gently pulls my plaits and calls me Rapunzel. I quite like this. I like my hair too. But I know pretty hair doesn't stop me looking weird. Well, not unless I turned into a real Rapunzel and grew it down to

my ankles and covered myself with it, like a great
furry hood and coat.

I'd like that. I could stay hidden inside. You're
always so *obvious* if you have a disability. You can't
hide behind the other kids or creep to a corner of the
classroom. You're always on display in your big
wheelchair, often with your helper beside you. You
can't whisper secrets when you have a voice
machine. You can't *have* secrets.

I had to get Wendy to tap in my worry on the
website as I can't reach the computer keys properly.
And when I wanted to look at the replies I couldn't
just wait for an appropriate moment and nip across
and have a quick glance. I had to get Wendy to
manoeuvre my wheelchair in and out the desks and
then click on all the right places on the screen.

I waited until after school
when everyone had gone
home. Mr Speed was still
there, but he pretended not
to notice what Wendy and
I were doing. He was
trying to construct some
kind of fairy-tale carriage
out of cardboard boxes
for the concert. He was
doing his best with gold

paint and old pram wheels but the audience might have to be kind and use their imagination. A girl called Lisa was painting scenery in a corner. She nodded to me shyly and then went on with her work. She seemed much more artistic than Mr Speed. She'd painted an all-purpose fairy-tale land with princesses with long golden hair and pink enchanted castles and wicked wizards swigging from their own bubbling cauldrons.

That's another thing I can't do. Paint. I know exactly how I want to do it in my head but it won't come out like that on the page. My hand just jerks and it all splodges. I won't even try now.

Mr Speed saw me staring at Lisa's scenery.

'It's good, isn't it, Natasha?'

'Very, very, very good,' I said with my voice machine. Wendy thought my finger had gone into spasm by the third 'very' and went to help me. I shook my head at her impatiently. Then I felt mean. It is so hard to have a helper all the time when you don't *want* to be helped.

Lisa looked up and smiled.

'Thank you,' she muttered, and carried on.

'The class members who lack specific talents are all in this mini-pantomime at the end of the concert.

That's what all this scenery is for. Oh lordy, this *wretched* concert,' said Mr Speed. He pressed down too hard on his fairy carriage and it collapsed. Mr Speed said a very rude word and then put his hand over his mouth. 'I hope you girls didn't hear that,' he said.

Lisa giggled. I giggled. Wendy giggled too.

'Why do I get involved year after year?' said Mr Speed. 'It's just one big worry.'

'Type your worry into the website!' I spoke slowly.

Mr Speed waited patiently and laughed when I was finished. 'Teachers aren't allowed to have worries,' he said.

He glanced ever so casually at the screen.

'What sort of comments has the latest worry attracted? I believe someone wants to be in the concert?'

'You know the someone is me,' I said.

'You're not daft, are you, Natasha?' said Mr Speed.

William *is* daft. He had typed in:

Why cant you bee in the consat? I am in it and I am useless at sining and dansing and stuff. But I am dooing cungring triks.

I blinked.

'What?'

'I think the lad means "conjuring",' said Mr Speed.

'I've helped him work out a routine with young Samantha.'

I blinked again.

'Can William *do* conjuring tricks?' Wendy asked doubtfully. She hasn't got to know all the children in Mr Speed's class – but you can't miss William.

'No, of course he can't. He drops all the cards and fails to pull out the ribbons and he can't produce the toy white rabbit from his cardboard top hat,' said Mr Speed, chuckling.

I decided maybe I didn't like Mr Speed after all.

'They will laugh at him,' I said. I can't put expression into my voice machine, but I tried to look disapproving.

'Don't frown at me, madam. They're *supposed* to laugh. William is *deliberately* mucking up his act. He's playing a totally useless conjuror. Well, he doesn't need to try hard, does he? And Samantha is going to get all gussied up in her ballet frock, being his beautiful blond assistant, and *she* will sort him out and do the trick each time.'

I nodded. I looked at another comment on the computer screen.

I wanted to sing a song with Holly but she's doing a dance with her little sister so I've got to sing on my own and my voice goes all wobbly and Mr Speed shouts, 'You're out of tune, lad' and makes it worse so I don't want to be in the concert.

113

'Oh dear,' said Mr Speed, reading over my shoulder. 'I do sound a bully, don't I? I'm not really that bad, am I, Natasha?'

'Yes!' I said.

Mr Speed laughed. Wendy laughed. Lisa looked up from her painting and laughed. I laughed too.

'Is everyone taking part in the concert?' Wendy asked.

'Not quite everyone. Lisa says she doesn't feel like performing. She's come to my rescue with the scenery. And hopefully she might help out with the props too.' Mr Speed gestured at the remains of his fairy carriage.

I asked Wendy to wheel me over to Lisa so I could have a closer look at her scenery. She parked me beside her and then went to have a little talk with Mr Speed. Probably about me. People are always having little talks about me and my progress – or lack of it. I'm OK at the difficult stuff. Ten out of ten in all lessons. I'm just useless at all the easy-peasy ordinary things everyone else takes for granted. I'm trapped in my baby body, unable to do anything for myself. Nought out of ten for walking, talking, going to the loo, combing my hair, whatever.

I like the way Lisa has her hair, short and spiky. It

looks seriously cool. Maybe it's time I had *my* hair cut?

I started telling her with my machine that I liked her hair. The mechanical voice made her jump and she blotched a bit of paint so that her princess got a red spot on the end of her nose to match her scarlet smile.

'Whoops!'

'Sorry I've spoilt your lady.' I wanted to say I'm sorry my mechanical voice sounds so stupid and I loved the way she's painted the beautiful fairy-tale princess but it would have taken too long.

'I think the wizard's put a curse on her. She's got spots. So have I, actually,' said Lisa. 'My mum says it's too much chocolate.'

My hand wasn't behaving itself because I wanted to make friends with Lisa so much. I had to make several stabs at it before I managed to say, 'I love chocolate.'

'I've got a Galaxy here,' said Lisa, fishing it out of her pocket with painty fingers. 'Do you want a bite?' Then she went pink. 'I mean . . . can you . . . can you eat, like, normally?'

'Try me!' I said.

She had the sense to break off a small square. She held it tentatively to my mouth. I tried *sooo* hard not to drool on her. I sucked the chocolate in and as I

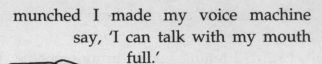 munched I made my voice machine say, 'I can talk with my mouth full.'

Lisa burst out laughing and gave me another piece of chocolate. She ate a square herself and then started sketching a house in a little wood at the right of her scenery.

'This is going to be the witch's gingerbread house, right? It's made out of sweets and chocolate and cakes and cookies. Maybe I could do it a bit like a collage, eh? Stick real little bits of chocolate on the roof?'

'Fruit gums for stained-glass windows and marshmallows for window ledges and Toblerone for a gable,' I spelt out endlessly. It took for ever but Lisa nodded at each word and calmly went on painting.

'That's so great, Natasha. If only you could paint too. What if we strapped a brush to your hand?'

'Too shaky.'

'How about your mouth?' Lisa gently put the end of her paintbrush in my mouth and then tried to push me nearer the desk where a piece of paper was set out. I saw Wendy step forward to help with the wheelchair but Mr Speed stopped her.

I tried hard, clenching my teeth. I know lots of people with severe disabilities use their mouths. Some really little kids at my special school can operate anything with a wriggle of their lips. But I find it incredibly difficult. It took me years to learn to drink with a *straw*, for goodness' sake. I'm hardly going to paint Mona Lisas with my mouth.

I had several goes but I kept dropping the stupid brush the minute it touched the paper. I thought Lisa would quickly get fed up with this lark but she was incredibly patient. I was the one who spat the brush out deliberately in disgust.

'Try again, Natasha,' said Mr Speed.

I *knew* he'd been watching us.

'You try,' I said with my machine. You can get away with being a bit cheeky when you've got disabilities.

'OK, I'll have a go,' said Mr Speed.

He sat in front of the piece of paper, stuck a paintbrush in his mouth, dabbled it – with difficulty – in a pot of pink paint and then tried to paint with it. He was too jerky and the paint much too runny. It spattered everywhere. Wendy was standing too near.

A spray landed on her nose, like pink freckles. Lisa and I fell about laughing. I almost did it literally, flopping sideways in my chair. Wendy was a good sport, laughing too as she hauled me upright.

"Orry, 'orry,' Mr Speed mumbled, his mouth still full of paintbrush. He had another go, frowning ferociously with concentration. He kept blotching, but by his fifth piece of paper he'd managed a lopsided daisy.

He removed the paintbrush and flourished his painting. Lisa and Wendy clapped and I pressed 'well done' on my talk machine. Mr Speed presented the painting to Wendy apologizing more coherently for spraying her with paint. Wendy went as pink as her freckles.

I caught Lisa's eye. She winked. We both giggled. Was there something going on between Wendy and *Mr Speed*?

Wendy was all too happy to stay behind with me after school. We sometimes popped round other days too.

My mum and dad were thrilled that I'd made a new friend.

'Ask Lisa if she wants to come to tea,' said Mum.

So I did, though I was a bit worried about it. Sometimes kids are happy to be your friend at school but they don't want to be real tell-you-everything-come-to-my-sleepover friends with someone like me. But Lisa looked really pleased. So Wendy drove us both home in the special adapted car and Lisa met my mum and my dad and my big sister Lois. I felt a bit bothered because they all baby me a bit, especially my dad. He always fusses round me, chucking me under the chin, tickling me, treating me like a fairy princess.

'My dad's a bit daft,' I said with my voice machine, when Lisa and I were in my room.

'Your dad's *lovely*,' said Lisa. She looked strangely sad. But she smiled again as she peered all round my room. 'Your room's so fantastic, Natasha!'

My room would be the front room or dining room in most people's houses, but it's my bedroom because it's downstairs so it saves Mum or Dad hauling me up and down every day. I didn't want it all frilly and little girly. I've got deep navy carpet and curtains and a navy and white checked duvet and a white table the right height for my wheelchair and a big white bookshelf unit with loads of brightly jacketed books and white bowls containing my cactus collection. There's a big crystal mobile hanging near the windows so there are rainbow sparkles on the white walls whenever the sun shines.

'Oh, I had one little crystal hanging up where we used to live,' Lisa said, touching the mobile very gently with one finger. 'But someone broke it when we moved.'

'I know a shop where—' I started to say with my voice machine, but Lisa was shaking her head.

'No, I don't want another. It wouldn't be the same.' Her voice went wobbly. 'Nothing's the same any more.'

I didn't say, 'Tell me.' The voice machine would bark it out like a robot order. I just looked *Tell me* with my eyes. Lisa came and sat beside me and started telling me all this sad, sad, sad stuff about her dad and how he drinks all the time now and hits her mum. Lisa cried a little. I wished I could reach out properly and give her a cuddle. My arms went flailing wildly all over the place, but Lisa understood. She grabbed one of my hands and we held onto each other tightly.

I tried to think what it must be like to be Lisa. My dad has a can or two of lager when he watches football on the television but I've never seen him *drunk*. He did come back acting a bit silly after his office party. He came into my room to kiss me goodnight – but he was just funny-drunk, singing songs to me and pretending to tie my plaits into tangles.

I can't ever imagine Dad hitting anyone. He's never once smacked Lois or me, even if we were really naughty, and he'd *never* hit Mum. He teases her a little bit if she gets bossy but she just laughs. I don't think I could bear it if I had Lisa's dad.

I couldn't tell her all this on my laborious machine. I just held onto her hand and she squeezed it tight.

'You won't tell anyone, will you, Natasha?' she said without thinking.

'As if!' I said with my machine, and we both laughed a little shakily.

'Did you tell Mr Speed?'

'No! And I was going to type a bit of it on the Worry Website and then I couldn't. Hey, I saw you putting something on the website, Natasha. What did you put? Or is it private?'

'No. It was silly. The concert. I wanted to be in it. Like sing? Dance? Ha ha.'

'I'm not in it either. I didn't feel like it so I said I'd paint the scenery.'

'But you *could* be in it.' I couldn't say it with the right emphasis but she understood.

'Yes, I suppose I could be the all-singing ever-dancing Lisa and warble and twirl and sing . . . ?'

'Don't worry, be happy!'

Lisa laughed.

I said it again, hitting the 'worry' word on my keyboard several times to make it sound like a funny little chorus.

Lisa looked at me.

'Do that again.'

I did.

'And you can keep on doing that? It doesn't hurt your hand, does it?'

'No, but it hurts my *ears*,' I said. 'It sounds weird.'

'It sounds perfect! Natasha, we'll do a song together at the concert. We can make up the verses, something about Mr Speed's website – and then we can sing it. I'll do the verses and each chorus is . . . ?'

'Worry worry worry worry!'

That's just what we did! The concert was *soooo* cool. The fairy-tale pantomime was great and everyone admired the spectacular scenery. But it was the star turns that went down really well. Holly and her little sister did a dance together wearing wonderful embroidered new dresses – they looked so cute. Greg sang a song about falling in love. He might have meant it to

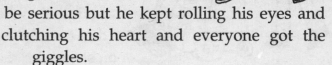

be serious but he kept rolling his eyes and clutching his heart and everyone got the giggles.

William and Samantha were the real surprise. I was getting nervous because it was nearly *our* turn and I so badly didn't want to let Lisa down. But I laughed so much at William mucking up his tricks and Samantha raising her eyebrows and tossing her hair and doing it for him that the tight feeling in my tummy disappeared. Everyone cheered and cheered William and Samantha. William's dad whistled and clapped like crazy and Samantha's dad was in tears. Samantha ran off the stage straight into his arms.

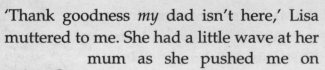

'Thank goodness *my* dad isn't here,' Lisa muttered to me. She had a little wave at her mum as she pushed me on stage.

Everyone went quiet and still. I knew they were all tense because of me. People who squirm around in wheelchairs don't usually perform on stage.

But once we got started it was OK. This is our *Worry Song*:

Worry worry worry worry
Worry worry worry worry
Have you got a worry
messing up your head?
Do you feel in a flurry?
Do you wish you were dead?

Worry worry worry worry
Worry worry worry worry
Do you have a secret fear?
Do you hate the way you look?
Do you shed a secret tear?
Seek an answer from a book?

Worry worry worry worry
Worry worry worry worry
Can't find a solution?
Can't get to sleep at night?
Do you worry about pollution,
starving people, men that fight?

Worry worry worry worry
Worry worry worry worry
Do your worries make you blush?
Are you scared to spit it out?
Do you blurt it in a rush?
Are you cast down in doubt?

Worry worry worry worry
Worry worry worry worry
Do you wet the bed?
Does your dad hit your mum?
Do you scream inside your head?
Does the pain make you numb?

Worry worry worry worry
Worry worry worry worry
Do you fuss about a spot?
Do you feel you are too fat?
Do you talk a lot of rot?
Do you feel a total prat?

Worry worry worry worry
Worry worry worry worry
Well, you know what to do
when your worries get you down.
The Worry Website's here for you
It will smooth out that frown.

Worry worry worry worry
Worry worry worry worry
Your friends will show they care
With comments frank but fond
It helps us all to share
And Mr Speed will wave his magic wand
To stop you going . . .
Worry worry worry worry
Worry worry worry worry
WORRY!

I said it was OK. It was more than OK. We were the glitter-girl stars of the show!

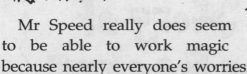

Mr Speed really does seem to be able to work magic because nearly everyone's worries have been sorted out. Even Mr Speed's. He sat hand in hand with Wendy throughout the entire concert!

Now flip the book to read

The Story of Tracy Beaker

BY JACQUELINE WILSON

ILLUSTRATED BY NICK SHARRATT

CORGI YEARLING BOOKS

THE STORY OF TRACY BEAKER and THE WORRY WEBSITE
A CORGI YEARLING BOOK 978 0 440 86735 5 (from January 2007)
0 440 86735 5

This edition first published in Great Britain for Scholastic by Corgi Yearling,
an imprint of Random House Children s Books, 2005

1 3 5 7 9 10 8 6 4 2

THE STORY OF TRACY BEAKER
First published in Great Britain in 1991 by Doubleday,
Corgi Yearling edition published 1992
Copyright © Jacqueline Wilson, 1991
Illustrations copyright © Nick Sharratt, 1991

THE WORRY WEBSITE
First published in Great Britain in 2002 by Doubleday,
Corgi Yearling edition published 2003
Copyright © Jacqueline Wilson, 2002
Lisa's Worry Copyright © Lauren Roberts, 2002
Illustrations copyright © Nick Sharratt, 1991

Papers used by Random House Children s Books are natural, recyclable
products made from wood grown in sustainable forests. The manufacturing
processes conform to the environmental regulations of the country of origin.

Corgi Yearling Books are published by Random House Children s Books,
61–63 Uxbridge Road, London W5 5SA,
a division of The Random House Group Ltd,
in Australia by Random House Australia (Pty) Ltd,
20 Alfred Street, Milsons Point, Sydney, NSW 2061, Australia,
in New Zealand by Random House New Zealand Ltd,
18 Poland Road, Glenfield, Auckland 10, New Zealand,
and in South Africa by Random House (Pty) Ltd,
Isle of Houghton, Corner Boundary Road & Carse O Gowrie,
Houghton 2198, South Africa

THE RANDOM HOUSE GROUP Limited Reg. No. 954009
www.kidsatrandomhouse.co.uk

A CIP catalogue record for this book is available from the British Library.

Printed and bound in Great Britain by
Cox & Wyman Ltd, Reading, Berkshire

To Bryony, David, Miranda,
Jason and Ryan

My Book About Me

ABOUT ME

My name is   Tracy Beaker

I am   10   years   2 months old.

My birthday is on   8 May. It's not fair, because that dopey Peter Ingham has his birthday then too, so we just got the one cake between us. And we had to hold the knife to cut the cake together. Which meant we only had half a wish each. Wishing is for babies anyway. They don't come true.

I was born at   some hospital somewhere. I looked cute when I was a little baby but I bet I yelled a lot.

I am cms **tall**. I don't know. I've tried measuring with a ruler but it keeps wobbling about and I can't reach properly. I don't want to get any of the other children to help me. This is my private book.

I weigh kgs. I don't know that either. Jenny has got scales in her bathroom but they're stones and pounds. I don't weigh many of them. I'm a little titch.

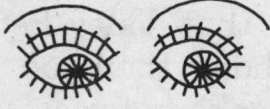

My eyes are black and I can make them go all wicked and witchy. I quite fancy being a witch. I'd make up all these incredibly evil spells and wave my wand and ZAP Louise's golden curls would all fall out and ZAP Peter Ingham's silly squeaky voice would get sillier and squeakier and he'd grow whiskers and a long tail and ZAP . . . there's not room on this bit of the page, but I've still got all sorts of ZAPs inside my head.

My hair is fair and very long and curly. I am telling fibs. It's dark and difficult and it sticks up in all the wrong places.

My skin is spotty when I eat a lot of sweets.

Stick a photo of yourself here

I'm not really cross-eyed. I was just pulling a silly face.

I started this book on   I don't know. Who cares what the date is? You always have to put the date at school. I got fed up with this and put 2091 in my Day Book and wrote about all these rockets and space ships and monsters legging it down from Mars to eat us all up, as if we'd all whizzed one hundred years into the future. Miss Brown didn't half get narked.

MORE THINGS ABOUT ME

Things I like

My lucky number is   7. So why didn't I get fostered by some fantastic rich family when I was seven then?

My favourite colour is   blood red, so watch out, ha-ha.

My best friend is Well, I've had heaps and heaps, but Louise has gone off with Justine and now I haven't got anyone just at the moment.

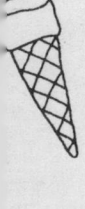

I like eating everything. I like birthday cake best. And any other kind of cake. And Smarties and Mars Bars and big buckets of popcorn and jelly spiders and Cornettos and Big Macs with french fries and strawberry milk shakes.

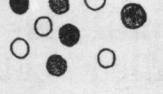

My favourite name is Camilla. There was a lovely little baby at this other home and that was her name. She was a really sweet kid with fantastic hair that I used to try to get into loads of little plaits and it must have hurt her sometimes but she never cried. She really liked me, little Camilla. She got fostered quick as a wink. I begged her foster mum and dad to bring her back to see me but they never did.

11

I like drinking   pints of bitter. That's a joke. I *have* had a sip of lager once but I didn't like it.

My favourite game is   playing with make-up. Louise and I once borrowed some from Adele who's got heaps. Louise was a bit boring and just tried to make herself look beautiful. I turned myself into an incredible vampire with evil shadowy eyes and blood dribbling down my chin. I didn't half scare the little ones.

My favourite animal is   Well, there's a rabbit called Lettuce at this home but it's a bit limp, like its name. It doesn't sit up and give you a friendly lick like a dog. I think I'd like a Rottweiler – and then all my enemies had better WATCH OUT.

My favourite TV programme is horror films.

Best of all I like being with my mum.

Things I don't like

the name Justine. Louise. Peter. Oh there's heaps and heaps of names I can't stand.

eating stew. Especially when it's got great fatty lumps in it. I used to have this horrid foster mother called Aunty Peggy and she was an awful cook. She used to make this slimy stew like molten sick and we were supposed to eat it all up, every single bit. Yuck.

Most of all I hate Justine. That Monster Gorilla. And not seeing my mum.

MY OWN FAMILY

Stick a photo of you and your family here

This was when I was a baby. See, I was sweet then. And this is my mum. She's ever so pretty. I wish I looked more like her.

The people in my own family are My mum. I don't have a dad. I lived with my mum when I was little and

we got on great but then she got this Monster Gorilla Boyfriend and I hated him and he hated me back and beat me up and so I had to be taken into care. No wonder my mum sent him packing.

My own family live at I'm not sure exactly where my mum lives now because she has to keep moving about because she gets fed up living in one place for long.

The phone number is Well, I don't know, do I? Funny though, I always used to bag this toy telephone in the playhouse at school and pretend I was phoning my mum. I used to have these long long conversations with her. They were just pretend of course, but I was only about five then and sometimes it got to be quite real.

Things about my family that I like I like my mum because she's pretty and good fun and she brings me lovely presents.

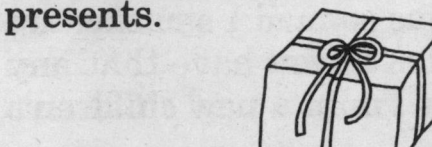

MY FOSTER FAMILY

There's no point filling this bit in. I haven't got a foster family at the moment.

I've had two. There was Aunty Peggy and Uncle Sid first of all. I didn't like them much and I didn't get on with the other kids so I didn't care when they got rid of me. I was in a children's home for a while and then I had this other couple. Julie and Ted. They were young and friendly and they bought me a bike and I thought it was all going to be great and I went to live with them and I was ever so good and did everything they said and I thought I'd be staying with them until my mum came to get me for good but then . . . I don't want to write about it. It ended up with me getting turfed out THROUGH NO FAULT OF MY OWN. I was so mad I smashed up the bike so I don't even have that any more. And now I'm in a new children's

home and they've advertised me in the papers but there weren't many takers and now I think they're getting a bit desperate. I don't care though. I expect my mum will come soon anyway.

MY SCHOOL

My school is called It's Kinglea Junior School. I've been to three other schools already. This one's OK I suppose.

My teacher is called Miss Brown. She gets cross if we just call her Miss.

Subjects I do Story-writing. Arithmetic. Games. Art. All sorts of things. And we do Projects only I never have the right stuff at the Home so I can't do it properly and get a star.

I like Story-writing best. I've written heaps of stories, and I do pictures for them too. I make some of them into books. I made Camilla a special baby book with big printed words and pictures of all the things she liked best, things like TEDDY and ICE-CREAM and YOUR SPECIAL FRIEND TRACY.

I also like Art. We use poster paints. We've got them at the Home too but they get all gungy and mucked up and the brushes are useless. They've got good ones at school. This is a painting I did yesterday. If I was a teacher I'd give it a gold star. *Two* gold stars.

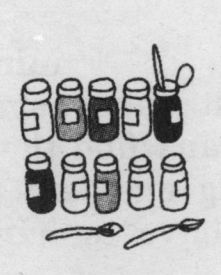

My class is   3a.

People in my class   I can't list all their names, I'd be here all night. I don't know some of them yet. There's not much point making friends because I expect I'll be moving on soon.

Other teachers   Oh, they're all boring. Who wants to write about them?

I get to school by   going in the Minibus. That's how all the kids in the home get to school. I'd sooner go in a proper car or walk it by myself but you're not allowed.

It takes   **hours**   **mins** It varies. Sometimes it takes ages because the little kids can't find their pencil cases and the big ones try to bunk off and we just have to hang about waiting.

Things I don't like about school

They all wear grey things, that's the uniform, and I've only got navy things from my last school. The teachers know why and I don't get into trouble but the other kids stare.

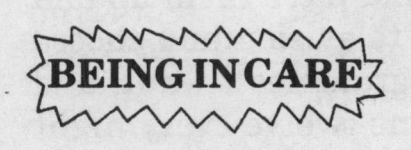

BEING IN CARE

My social worker is called Elaine and sometimes she's a right pain, ha-ha.

We talk about all sorts of boring things.

But I don't like talking about my mum. Not to Elaine. What I think about my mum is private.

IF I WAS . .

older, I would live in this really great modern house all on my own, and I'd have my own huge bedroom with all my own things, special bunk beds just for me so that I'd always get the top one and a Mickey Mouse alarm clock like Justine's and my own giant set of poster paints and I'd have some felt tips as well and no-one would ever get to borrow them and mess them up and I'd have my own television and choose exactly what programmes I want, and I'd stay up till gone twelve every night and I'd eat at McDonald's every single day and I'd have a big fast car so I could whizz off and visit my mum whenever I wanted.

a policeman, I would arrest the Monster Gorilla and I'd lock him up in prison for ever.

a kitten, I would grow very long claws and sharp teeth and scratch and bite everyone so they'd get really scared of me and do everything I say.

yelled at, I would yell back.

invisible, I would spy on people.

very tall, I would stamp on people with my great big feet.

very rich, I would buy my own house and then . . . I've done all that bit. I'm getting fed up writing all this. What's on the next page?

MY OWN STORY

Use this space to write your story

THE STORY OF TRACY BEAKER

Once upon a time there was a little girl called
Tracy Beaker. That sounds a bit stupid, like
the start of a soppy fairy story. I can't stand
fairy stories. They're all the same. If you're
very good and very beautiful with long golden
curls then, after sweeping up a few cinders
or having a long kip in a cobwebby palace,
this prince comes along and you live happily
ever after. Which is fine if you happen to
be a goodie-goodie and look gorgeous. But
if you're bad and ugly then you've got no
chance whatsoever. You get given a silly name
like *Rumpelstiltskin* and nobody invites you to
their party and no-one's ever grateful even
when you do them a whopping great favour.
So of course you get a bit cheesed off with this
sort of treatment. You stamp your feet in a
rage and fall right through the floorboards or
you scream yourself into a frenzy and you get
locked up in a tower and they throw away the
key.

24

I've done a bit of stamping and screaming in my time.

And I've been locked up heaps of times. Once they locked me up all day long. And all night. That was at the first Home, when I wouldn't settle because I wanted my mum so much. I was just little then but they still locked me up. I'm not fibbing. Although I do have a tendency to tell a few fibs now and again. It's funny, Aunty Peggy used to call it Telling Fairy Stories.

I'd say something like — 'Guess what, Aunty Peggy, I just met my mum in the back garden and she gave me a ride in her flash new sports car and we went down the shopping arcade and she bought me my very own huge bottle of scent, that posh *Poison* one, just like the bottle Uncle Sid gave you for your birthday, and I was messing about

with it, playing Murderers, and the bottle sort of tipped and it's gone all over me as I expect you've noticed, but it's my scent not yours. I don't know what's happened to yours. I think one of the other kids took it.'

You know the sort of thing. I'd make it dead convincing but Aunty Peggy wouldn't even listen properly. She'd just shake her head at me and get all cross and red and say, 'Oh Tracy, you naughty girl, you're Telling Fairy Stories again.' Then she'd give me a smack.

Foster mothers aren't supposed to smack you at all. I told Elaine that Aunty Peggy used to smack me and Elaine sighed and said, 'Well sometimes, Tracy, you really do ask for it.' Which is a lie in itself. I have never in my life said 'Aunty Peggy, please will you give me a great big smack.' And her smacks really hurt too, right on the back of your leg where it stings most. I didn't like that Aunty Peggy at all. If I was in a real fairy story I'd put a curse on her. A huge wart right on the end of her nose? Frogs and toads coming wriggling out of her mouth every time she tries to speak? No, I 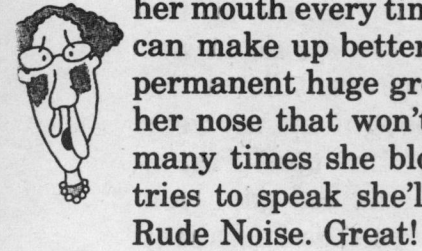 can make up better than that. She can have permanent huge great bogeys hanging out of her nose that won't go away no matter how many times she blows it, and whenever she tries to speak she'll make this terribly loud Rude Noise. Great!

Oh dear. You can't win. Elaine, my stupid old social worker, was sitting beside me when I started writing THE STORY OF TRACY BEAKER and I got the giggles making up my brilliant curses for Aunty Peggy and Elaine looked surprised and said, 'What are you laughing at, Tracy?'

I said, 'Mind your own business' and she said, 'Now Tracy' and then she looked at what I'd written which is a bit of a cheek seeing as it's supposed to be very private. She sighed when she got to the Aunty Peggy part and said, 'Really Tracy!' and I said, 'Yes, really, Elaine.' And she sighed again and her lips moved for a moment or two. That's her taking a deep breath and counting up to ten. Social workers are supposed to do that when a child is being difficult. Elaine ends up doing an awful lot of counting when she's with me.

When she got to ten she gave me this big false smile. Like this.

'Now look, Tracy,' said Elaine. 'This is your own special book about you, something that you're going to keep for ever. You don't want to spoil it by writing all sorts of silly cheeky rude things in it, do you?'

I said, 'It's my life and it hasn't been very special so far, has it, so why shouldn't I write any old rubbish?'

Then she sighed again, but sympathetically this time, and she put her arm round me and said, 'Hey, I know you've had a hard time, but *you're* very special. You know that, don't you?'

I shook my head and tried to wriggle away.

'Yes, you are, Tracy. Very very special,' Elaine said, hanging on to me.

'Then if I'm so very very special how come no-one wants me?' I said.

'Oh dear, I know it must have been very disappointing for you when your second placement went wrong, love, but you mustn't let it depress you too much. Sooner or later you'll find the perfect placement.'

'A fantastic rich family?'

'Maybe a family. Or maybe a single person, if someone really suitable came along.'

I gave her this long look. 'You're single, Elaine. And I bet you're suitable. So why don't you foster me, eh?'

It was her turn to wriggle then.

'Well, Tracy. You know how it is. I mean, I've got my job. I have to deal with lots of children.'

'But if you fostered me you could stop bothering with all the others and just look after me. They give you money if you foster. I bet they'd give you lots extra because I'm difficult, and I've got behaviour problems and all that. How about it, Elaine? It would be fun, honest it would.'

'I'm sure it would be lots of fun, Tracy, but I'm sorry, it's just not on,' Elaine said.

She tried to give me a big hug but I pushed her hard.

'I was only joking,' I said. 'Yuck. I couldn't stand the thought of living with you. You're stupid and boring and you're all fat and wobbly, I'd absolutely hate the idea of you being my foster mum.'

'I can understand why you're angry with me, Tracy,' said Elaine, trying to look cool and calm, but sucking in her stomach all the same.

I told her I wasn't a bit angry, though I shouted as I said it. I told her I didn't care a bit, though I had these silly watery eyes. I didn't cry though. I don't *ever* cry. Sometimes people think I do, but it's my hay fever.

'I expect you're going to think up all sorts of revolting curses for me now,' said Elaine.

'I'm doing it right this minute,' I told her.
'OK,' she said.

'You always say OK,' I told her. 'You know: OK, that's fine with me, if that's what you want I'm not going to make a fuss; OK Tracy, yes I know you've got this socking great axe in your hand and you're about to chop off my head because you're feeling angry with me, but OK, if that's the way you feel, I'm not going to get worried about it because I'm this super-cool social worker.'

She burst out laughing then.

'No-one can stay super-cool when you're around, Tracy,' she said. 'Look kiddo, you write whatever you want in your life story. It's your own book, after all.'

So that's that. This is my own book and I can write whatever I want. Only I'm not quite sure what I do want, actually. Maybe Elaine *could* help after all. She's over the other side of the sitting-room, helping that wet Peter with his book. He hasn't got a clue. He's filling it all in *so* slowly and *so* seriously, not writing it but printing it with that silly blotchy biro of his, trying to do it ever so carefully but failing miserably, and now he's smudged some of it so it looks a mess anyway.

I've just called Elaine but she says she's got to help Peter for a bit. The poor little petal is

getting all worried in case he puts the wrong answers, as if it's some dopey intelligence test. I've done heaps of them, intelligence tests. They're all ever so easy-peasy. I can do them quick as a wink. They always expect kids in care to be as thick as bricks, but I get a hundred out of a hundred nearly every time. Well, they don't tell you the answers, but I bet I do.

TRACY BEAKER IS A STUPID SHOW-OFF AND THIS IS THE SILLIEST LOAD OF RUBBISH I'VE EVER READ AND IF SHE'S SO SUPER-INTELLIGENT HOW COME SHE WETS HER BED LIKE A BABY ?

Ignore the stupid scribble up above. It's all lies anyway. It's typical. You can't leave anything for two minutes in this rotten place without one of the other kids spoiling it. But I never thought anyone would stoop so low as to write in my own private life story. And I know who did it too. I know, Justine Littlewood, and you just wait. I'm going to get you.

I went over to rescue Elaine from that boring wimpy little Peter and I had a little peer into his book and I nearly fell over, because you'll never guess who he's put as his best friend. Me. *Me!*

'Is this some sort of joke?' I demanded.
He went all red and mumbly and tried to
hide what he'd put, but I'd already seen it.
My best friend is Tracy Beaker. It was down
there on the page in black and white. Well,
not your actual black and white, more your
smudgy blue biro, but you know what I mean.

'Go away and stop pestering poor Peter,'
Elaine said to me.

'Yes, but he's putting absolute rubbish in
his book, Elaine, and it's stupid. I'm not Peter
Ingham's best friend!'

'Well, I think it's very nice that Peter
wants you to be his friend,' said Elaine. She
pulled a funny face. 'There's no accounting for
taste.'

'Oh, ha-ha. Why did you put that, Peter?'

Peter did a little squeak about sharing birthdays and so that made us friends.

'It does *not* make us friends, dumbo,' I declared.

Elaine started getting on at me then, saying I was being nasty to poor little Peetie-Weetie and if I couldn't be friendly why didn't I just push off and get on with my own life story? Well, when people tell me to push off I generally try to stick to them like glue, just to be annoying, so that's what I did.

And then Jenny called me into the kitchen because she made out she wanted a hand getting the lunch ready, but that was just a *ploy*. Jenny doesn't smack. She doesn't even often tell you off. She just uses ploys and tries to distract you. It sometimes works with the thicker kids but it usually has no effect whatsoever on me. However, I quite like helping in the kitchen because you can generally nick a spoonful of jam or a handful of raisins when Jenny's back is turned. So I went along to the kitchen and helped her put an entire shoal of fish fingers under the double grill while she got the chip pan bubbling. Fish fingers don't taste so great when they're raw. I tried nibbling just to see. I don't know why they're called fish *fingers*. They don't have fingers, do they? They ought to be fish *fins*. That Aunty

33

Peggy used to make this awful milk pudding called tapioca which had these little slimy bubbly bits and I told the other kids that they were fish eyes. And I told the really little ones that marmalade is made out of goldfish and they believed that too.

When Jenny started serving out the fish fingers and chips, I went back into the sitting-room to tell everyone that lunch was ready. And I remember seeing Louise and Justine hunched up in a corner, giggling over something they'd got hidden. I don't know. I *am* highly intelligent, I truly wasn't making that up, and yet it was a bit thick of me not to twig what they were up to. Which was reading my own life story and then scribbling all over it.

A little twit like Peter Ingham would tell, but I'm no tell-tale tit. I shall simply get my own back. I shall think long and carefully for a suitable horrible revenge. I don't half hate that Justine. Before she came Louise and I were best friends and we did everything together and, even though I was still dumped in a rotten children's home, it really wasn't so bad. Louise and I made out we were sisters and we had all these secrets and—

One of these secrets was about a certain small problem that I have. A night-time problem. I've got my own room and so it was always a private problem that only Jenny

and I knew about. Only to show Louise we were the bestest friends ever I told her about it. I knew it wasn't a sensible move right from the start because she giggled, and she used to tease me about it a bit even when we were still friends. And then she went off with Justine and I'd sometimes worry that she might tell on me, but I always convinced myself she'd never ever stoop that low. Not Louise.

But she has told. She's told Justine, my worst enemy. So what am I going to do to her? Any ideas ticking away inside my head?

Well, I could beat her up.

Tick, tick, tick.
I could deliver a karate chop death blow.

Tick, tick, tick.
I could get my mum to come in her car and
run her over, squashing her hedgehog-flat.

Tick, tick, tick. Hey! Tick tock. Tick tock. *I* know. And I also know I'm not leaving this book hanging about. From now on I shall carry it on my person. So, ha-ha, sucks boo to you, Justine Littlewood. Oh you're going to get it. Yes you are, yes you are, tee-hee.

I'm writing this at midnight. I can't put the light on because Jenny might still be prowling about and I don't want *another* ding-dong with her, thanks very much. I'm making do with a torch, only the battery's going, so there's just this dim little glow and I can hardly see what I'm doing. I wish I had something to eat. In all those Enid Blyton school stories they always have midnight feasts. The food sounds a bit weird, sardines and condensed milk, but I could murder a Mars Bar right this minute. Imagine a Mars Bar as big as this bed. Imagine licking it, gnawing away at a corner, scooping out the soft part with both fists. Imagine the wonderful chocolatey smell. I'm slavering at the thought. Yes, that's what those little marks are on the page. Slavers. I don't cry. I don't *ever* cry.

I acted as if I didn't care less when Jenny had a real go at me. And I don't.

'I think you really do care, Tracy,' she said, in that silly sorrowful voice. 'Deep down I think you're really very sorry.'

'That's just where you're wrong,' I insisted.

'Come off it now. You must know how you'd feel if your mother had bought you a special present and one of the other kids spoilt it.'

As she said that I couldn't help remembering being in the first Home, long before the dreaded Aunty Peggy or that mean hateful unfair Julie and Ted. My mum came to see me and she'd brought this doll, a doll almost as big as me, with long golden curls and a bright blue lacy dress to match her big blue eyes. I'd never liked dolls all that much but I thought this one was wonderful. I called her Bluebell and I undressed her right down to her frilly white knickers and dressed her up again and brushed her blonde curls and made her blink her big blue eyes, and at night she'd lie in my bed and we'd have these cosy little chats and she'd tell me that Mum was coming back really soon, probably tomorrow, and—

OK, that sort of thing makes me want to puke now but I was only little then and I didn't know any better. The housemother let me cart Bluebell all over the place but she tried to make me give the other kids a go at playing with her. Well, I wasn't going to let that lot maul her about, so of course I didn't let them hold her. But I came unstuck when I started school. You weren't allowed to

38

take toys to school, only on Friday afternoons. I cried and fought but they wouldn't let me. So I had to start leaving Bluebell at home. I'd tuck her up in my bed with her eyes closed, pretending she was asleep, and then when I got home from school I'd charge upstairs into our crummy little dormitory and wake her up with a big hug. Only one day I woke her up and I got the shock of my life. Her eyelids snapped open but her blue eyes had vanished inside her head. Some rotten lousy pig had given them a good poke. I couldn't stand it, seeing those creepy empty sockets. She stopped being my friend. She just scared me.

The housemother took Bluebell off to this dolls' hospital and they gave her some new eyes. They were blue too, but not the same bright blue, and they didn't blink properly either. They either got stuck altogether or they flashed up and down all the time, making her look silly and fluttery. But I didn't really care then. She was spoilt. She wasn't the same Bluebell. She didn't talk to me any more.

I never found out which kid had done it. The housemother said it was A Mystery. Just One Of Those Things.

Jenny didn't call it a mystery when Justine went sobbing to her because her silly old Mickey Mouse alarm clock had got broken.

Clocks break all the time. It's not as if it's a really flash expensive clock. If I'd been Jenny I'd have told Justine to stop making such a silly fuss. I'd have stopped up my ears when that sneaky little twerp started going on about me. 'I bet I know who did it too, Jenny. *That Tracy Beaker.*'

Yes, she sneaked on me. And Jenny listened, because she came looking for me. She had to look quite a long time. I kind of suspected what was coming, so I cleared off. I didn't try to hide in the house or the garden like one of the little kids. I'm not that dumb. They can flush you out in five minutes no matter where you are. No, I skipped it out the back door and down the road and went for a wander round the town.

It was great. Yes, I had the most amazing time. First I went to McDonald's and had a Big Mac and french fries with a strawberry milk shake and then I went to the pictures

and saw this really funny film and I laughed so much I fell out of my seat and then I went off with this whole crowd of friends to an amusement arcade and I kept winning the jackpot on the fruit machines and then we all went off to this party and I drank a whole bottle of wine and it was great, it just tasted like lemonade, and this girl there, we made friends and she asked me if I'd like to stay the night, sharing her twin beds in this fantastic pink and white room, in fact she said I could stay there permanently if I really wanted and so I said . . .

I said: 'No thanks, I'd sooner go back to my crummy children's home.' ?

41

Of course I didn't say that. Well, she didn't say it either. I sort of made her up. And her party. I didn't go down the amusement arcade. Or to the pictures. Or McDonald's. I *would* have done, but I couldn't, on account of the fact I ran off with no cash whatsoever.

I said I tell fibs sometimes. It makes things more interesting. I mean, what's the point of writing what I really did? Which was loaf about the town feeling more and more fed up. The only thing I could think of to do was sit in the bus shelter. It got a bit boring. I pretended I was waiting for a bus and I tried to think of all the places I'd like to go to. But that began to depress me because I started thinking about Watford, where my mum said she lived. And last year I got all the right money together (which created a few problems afterwards as I sort of borrowed it without asking) and sussed out the journey and got all these trains and buses and all the rest of it, so that I could pay my mum a visit and give her a lovely surprise. Only it was me that got the surprise because she wasn't there, and the people who lived in that house said she'd moved on about six months ago and they didn't have a clue where she'd gone now.

So it's going to take a bit of organized searching to find her again. I could catch a different bus every day for the rest of my life

and maybe not find her. It's hard when you haven't got a clue where to look.

I was still scrunched up in the bus shelter when a familiar white Minivan hoved into view. It was Mike, come looking for me. Mike looks after us with Jenny. He isn't half a bore. He doesn't often get cross but he whinges on about Rules and Responsibility and a whole lot of other rubbish.

So by the time I'd got back to the Home I was sick to death of the subject, but then Jenny came into my bedroom and *she* started. And she assumed it was me that broke Justine's clock though she had no proof whatsoever. I told her so, and said she just

liked picking on me, and it wasn't fair. She said I'd feel better if I owned up to breaking Justine's clock and then went to say sorry to her. I said she had to be joking. I wasn't the slightest bit sorry and anyway I didn't didn't *didn't* break Justine's rotten clock.

That isn't necessarily a fib. I don't absolutely one hundred percent *know* that I broke it. All right, I did go into her bedroom when she was in the bathroom, and I did pick up the clock to look at it. Well, she's always going on about it because she's got this boring thing about her dad. She makes out he's so flipping special when he hardly ever comes to see her. The only thing he's ever given her is that stupid tinny old alarm clock. I wanted to look at it to see if it was really so special. Well, it wasn't. I bet he just got it from Woolworth's. And it certainly wasn't made very carefully because when I twiddled the knobs to make the little Mickey on the end of the hands go whizzing round and round he couldn't keep it up for very long. There was this sudden whir and clunk and then the hand fell off altogether and Mickey fell too, with his little paws in the air, dead.

But he might have been about to take his last gasp anyway. That hand might well have fallen off the next time Justine touched the stupid clock to wind it up.

I'm not going to say sorry no matter what.
I wish I could get to sleep.
I'll try counting sheep . . .

I *still* can't get to sleep and it's the middle
of the night now and it's rotten and I keep
thinking about my mum. I wish she'd come
and get me. I wish anyone would come and
get me. Why can't I ever get a good foster
family? That Aunty Peggy and Uncle Sid were
lousy. But then I could suss them out and tell
they were lousy right from the start. Anyone
who smacks hard and serves up frogspawn for
your pudding is certainly not an ideal aunty.
But last time, when I got fostered by Julie
and Ted, I really thought it was all going to
work out happily ever after, and that it was
my turn to be the golden princess instead of
a *Rumpelstiltskin*.

They were great at first, Julie and Ted. That's what I called them right from the start. They didn't want to be a prissy aunty and uncle. And Julie said she didn't want me to call her Mum because I already had a mum. I thought such a lot of Julie when she said that. She wasn't exactly my idea of a glamorous foster mum – she had this long wispy brown hair and she wore sludge-coloured smocky things and sandals – and Ted looked a bit of a wimp too with his glasses and his beard and weirdo comfy walking shoes, not so much

Hush Puppy as Shut-your-face Hound-Dog –
but I thought they were the sort of couple you
could really trust. Ha!

Because I went to live with them and
I thought we were getting on really great,
though they were a bit boringly strict about
stuff like sweets and bedtimes and horror
videos, but then Julie started to wear bigger
smocks than ever and lolled about on the sofa
and Ted got all misty-eyed behind his glasses
and I started to realize that something was
up. And so I asked them what it was and
they hedged and pulled faces at each other
and then they looked shifty and told me that
everything was fine and I knew they were
lying. Things weren't fine at all.

They didn't even have the guts to tell me
themselves. They left it to Elaine. She'd only
just started to be my social worker then (I've
had heaps because they kept moving around
and leaving me behind and I got passed on
like a parcel). I wasn't that keen on Elaine
in those days. In fact I was really narked
with her, because I'd had this man social
worker Terry before her and he used to call
me Smartie and he used to give me the odd
tube of Smarties too, and I felt Elaine was a
very poor substitute.

I wish I hadn't thought of those Smarties.
I wish I had some now, I'm simply starving.

I'm sure Elaine marked me down as Sulky and Non-co-operative in her little notebook. The day she told me the Julie and Ted Bombshell I'm sure she scribbled TRACY TOTALLY GOB-SMACKED. Because Julie was having her own baby, after years of thinking she couldn't have any kids.

I didn't get it at first.

'So what's the problem, Elaine?' I said. 'We'll be a proper family then, four of us instead of three.'

Elaine was having difficulties finding the right words. She kept opening her mouth and closing it again, not saying a sausage.

'You look just like a fish when you do that, did you know?' I said cheekily, because my heart was starting to hammer hard against my chest and I knew that when Elaine eventually got the words out I wouldn't like the sound of them.

'The thing is, Tracy . . . Well, Julie and Ted have loved fostering you, and they've got very fond of you, but . . . you see, now they're having their own baby they feel that they're not really going to be able to cope.'

'Oh, I get it,' I said, in this jokey silly voice. 'So they're going to give the boring old baby away because they can't cope with it. And keep me. Because they had me first, didn't they?'

'Tracy—'

'They're not really going to dump me, are they?'

'They still very much want to keep in touch with you and—'

'So why can't I go on living with them? Look, I'll help all I can. Julie doesn't need to worry. I'll be just like a second mum to this baby. I know all what to do. I can give it its bottle and change its soggy old nappy and thump it on its back to bring up its wind. I'm dead experienced where babies are concerned.'

'Yes, I know, Tracy. But that's the trouble. You see, when Julie and Ted first fostered you, we did tell them a bit about your background, and the trouble you had in your first foster home. You know, when you shut the baby up in the cupboard—'

'That was. Steve. And he wasn't a baby. He was a foul little toddler, and he kept mucking up our bedroom so I tidied him up into the cupboard just for a bit so I could get everything straightened out.'

'And there was the ghost game that got totally out of hand—'

'Oh that! All those little kids *loved* that game. I was ever so good at finding the right hiding places and then I'd start an eerie sort of moan and then I'd jump out at them, wearing this old white sheet.'

49

'And everyone got scared silly.'

'No they didn't. They just squealed because they were excited. *I* was the one who should have been scared, because they were all the ghost-busters you see, and I was the poor little ghost and—'

'OK, OK, but the point is, Tracy, it makes it plain in your records that you don't always get on well with little children.'

'That's a whopping great lie! What about Camilla? I looked after her at that children's home and she loved me, she really did.'

'Yes, I'm sure that's true, Tracy, but— Well, the thing is, Julie and Ted still feel they don't want to take any chances. They're worried you might feel a bit uncomfortable with a baby in the house.'

'So they're pushing me out?'

'But like I said, they still want to keep in touch with you and maybe take you out for tea sometimes.'

'No way,' I said. 'I don't want to see them ever again.'

'Oh Tracy, that's silly. That's just cutting off your own nose to spite your face,' said Elaine.

That's such a daft expression. How on earth would you go about it?

It wouldn't half hurt.

It hurt a lot leaving Julie and Ted's.

They wanted me to stay for a few months but I couldn't clear out of there quick enough. So here I am in this dump. They've tried to see me twice but I wasn't having any of it. I don't want any visitors, thanks very much. Apart from my mum. I wonder where she is. And why didn't she leave a forwarding address at that last place? And how will she ever get to find me here? Yeah, that's the problem. I bet she's been trying and trying to get hold of me, but she doesn't know where to look. Last time I saw her I was at Aunty Peggy's. I bet Mum's been round to Aunty Peggy's and I bet that silly old smacking-machine wouldn't tell her where I'd gone. So I bet my mum got really mad with her. And if she found out just how many times that Aunty Peggy smacked me then wow, ker-pow, splat, bang, I bet my mum would really let her have it.

I don't half want my mum.

I know why I can't sleep. It's because I'm so starving hungry, that's why. Crying always makes me hungry. Not that I've been crying now. I don't *ever* cry.

I think maybe I'll try slipping down to the kitchen. Jenny's bound to be fast asleep by now. Yeah, that's what I'll do.

I'm back. I've had my very own midnight feast. And it was absolutely delicious too. Well, it wasn't bad. I couldn't find any chocolate, of course, and that was what I really fancied. But I found an opened packet of cornflakes and got stuck into them, and then I tried raiding the fridge. There weren't too many goodies. I didn't go a bundle on tomorrow's uncooked mince or yesterday's cold custard, but I poked my finger in the butter and then dabbled it in the sugar bowl and that tasted fine. I did quite a lot of poking and dabbling actually. I know Jenny might notice so I got my little finger nail and drew these weeny lines like teethmarks and then did some paw prints all over the butter, so she'd think it was a mouse. Mice do eat butter, don't they? They like cheese, which is the same sort of thing. Of course this is going to have to be a mountaineering mouse, armed with ice-pick and climbing boots, able to trek

up the grim north face of the Frigidaire. And then it's got to develop Mighty Mouse muscles to prise open the door of the fridge to get at the feast inside.

Maybe Jenny will still be a teensy bit suspicious. But I can't help that. At least she didn't catch me while I was noshing away at my midnight feast.

Someone else did though. Not in the kitchen. Afterwards, when I was sneaking up the stairs again. They're very dark, these stairs, and they take a bit of careful negotiating. One of the little kids is quite likely to leave a teddy or a rattle or a building brick halfway up and you can come an awful cropper and wake the entire household. So I was feeling my way very very cautiously when I heard this weird little moaning sound coming from up on the landing. So I looked up, sharpish, and I could just make out this pale little figure, all white and trailing, and it was so exactly like a ghost that I opened my mouth to scream.

But Tracy Beaker has a lot of bottle. I'm not scared of anybody. Not even ghosts. So I clapped my hand over my mouth to stop the scream and pattered right on up the stairs to confront this puny little piece of ectoplasm. Only it wasn't a ghost after all. It was just snivelling drivelling Peter Ingham, clutching some sheets.

'Whatever are you up to, creep?' I whispered.

'Nothing,' Peter whispered back.

'Oh sure. You just thought you'd take your sheets for a walk in the middle of the night,' I said.

Peter flinched away from me.

'You've wet them, haven't you?' I said.

'No,' Peter mumbled. He's a useless liar.

'Of course you've wet them. And you've been trying to wash them out in the bathroom, I know. So that people won't guess.'

'Oh don't tell, Tracy, please,' Peter begged.

'What do you take me for? I'm no tell-tale,' I said. 'And look, you don't have to fuss. Just get Jenny on her own in the morning and whisper to her. She'll sort it all out for you. She doesn't get cross.'

'Really?'

'Truly. And what you do now, you get yourself some dry sheets from the airing

cupboard, right? And some pyjamas. Goodness, you don't know anything, do you? How long have you been in care?'

'Three months, one week, two days,' said Peter.

'Is that all? I've been in and out of care nearly all my life,' I said, getting the sheets for him. 'So why are you here now then? Your mum and dad get fed up with you? Can't say as I blame them.'

'They died when I was little. So I lived with my nan. But then she got old and then– then she died too,' Peter mumbled. 'And I didn't have anyone else so I had to come here. And I don't like it.'

'Well, of course you don't like it. But this is a lot better than most children's homes. You ought to have tried some of the places I've been in. They lock you up and they beat you and they practically starve you to death and then when they do give you meals it's absolutely disgusting, they pretend it's meat but it's really chopped up worms and dried dog's muck and— '

'Shut up, Tracy,' Peter said, holding his stomach.

'Who are you telling to shut up?' I said, but not really fiercely. 'Go on, you'd better shove off back to your room. And put your

dry pyjamas on. You're shivering.'

'OK, Tracy. Thanks.' He paused, fidgeting and fumbling with his sheets. 'I wish you would be my friend, Tracy.'

'I don't really bother making friends,' I said. 'There's not much point, because my mum's probably coming to get me soon and then I'll be living with her so I won't need any friends here.'

'Oh,' said Peter, and he sounded really disappointed.

'Still. I suppose you can be my friend just for now,' I said.

I don't know why I said it. Who wants to be lumbered with a silly little creep like that? I'm too kind-hearted, that's my trouble.

There wasn't much point in getting to sleep, because when I did eventually nod off I just had these stupid nightmares. It's as if there's a video inside my head and it switches itself on the minute my eyes close and I keep hoping it's going to be showing this great comedy that'll have me in stitches but then the creepy music starts and I know I'm in for it. Last night was the Great Horror Movie of all time. I was stuck in the dark somewhere and there was something really scary coming up quick behind me so I had to run like

mad. Then I got to this big round pool and there were these stepping stones with people perching on them and I jumped on to the first one and there was no room at all because that fat Aunty Peggy was spread all over it. I tried to cling to her but she gave me a big smack and sent me flying. So then I jumped on to the next stepping stone and Julie and Ted were there and I tried to grab hold of them but they just turned their backs on me and didn't even try to catch me when I fell and so I had to try to reach the next stepping stone but I was in the water doing my doggy-paddle

and it was getting harder and harder, and every time I swam to a stepping stone all these people prodded at me with sticks and pushed me away and I kept going under the water and . . .

. . . and then I woke up and I know that whenever I dream about water it spells Trouble with a capital T. I had to make my own dash to the airing cupboard and the laundry basket. I was unfortunate enough to bump into Justine too. She didn't look as if she'd slept much either. Her eyes seemed a bit on the red side. I couldn't help feeling a bit mean then, in spite of everything. So I gave her this big smile and I said, 'I'm sorry about what happened to your alarm clock, Justine.'

I didn't exactly tell her that *I* did it. Because I still don't know that it really was me. And anyway, I'd be a fool to admit it, wouldn't I? But I told her that I was still sorry, just like Jenny had suggested.

Only there's no point trying to be nice to pigs like Justine Littlewood. She didn't smile back and graciously accept my apologies.

'You'll be even sorrier when I've finished with you, Tracy Beaker,' she hissed. 'And what have you been doing, eh? Wet the bed again? Baby!' She hissed a lot more too. Stupid insulting things. I'm not going to

waste my time writing them all down. Words can't hurt me anyway. Only I can't help being just a bit worried about that threat. What's she going to do to get her own back for the clock? If only we had poxy locks on our bedroom doors. Still, at least we've got separate bedrooms in this Home, even though they're weeny like cupboards.

It's new policy. Children in care need their own space. And I want to stay in my own space, doing all this writing, but Jenny has just put her head round my door and told me to buzz out into the garden with the others. And I said No Fear. Being in a Home is lousy at the best of times, but I just can't stick it in the school holidays when you're all cooped up together and the big ones bully you and the little ones pester you and the ones your own age gang up on you and have secrets together and call you names.

'How's about trying to make it up with Justine?' Jenny suggested, coming to sit on my bed.

So I snorted and told her she was wasting her time, and more to the point, she was wasting *my* time, because I wanted to get on with my writing.

'You've done ever such a lot, Tracy,' said Jenny, looking at all these pages. 'We'll be running out of paper soon.'

'Then I'll use the backs of birthday cards. Or bog roll. Anything. I'm inspired, see. I can't stop.'

'Yes, you've really taken to this writing. Going to be a writer when you grow up, eh?'

'Maybe.' I hadn't thought about it before. I was always sure I was going to be on telly with my own chat show. THE TRACY BEAKER EXPERIENCE and I'd walk out on to this stage in a sparkly dress and all the studio audience would clap and cheer and all these really famous celebrities would fight tooth and nail to get on my show to speak to me. But I reckon I could write books too.

'Tell you what, Tracy. We've got a real writer coming round some time this afternoon. You could ask her for a few tips.'

'What's she coming for?'

'Oh, she's doing this article for a magazine about children in care.'

'Oh that boring old stuff,' I said, pretending to yawn but inside I start fizzing away.

I wouldn't mind my story being written up in some magazine. A book would be better of course, but maybe that could come later. I'd have to be careful what she said about me though. Elaine the Pain made a right mess of my newspaper advert. I was Child of the Week in the local paper. If she'd only let me write it I'd have been bowled over by people rushing to adopt dear little Tracy Beaker. I know just how to present myself in the right sort of way.

TRACY BEAKER

HAVE YOU A PLACE IN YOUR HEARTS FOR DEAR LITTLE TRACY? BRILLIANT AND BEAUTIFUL, THIS LITTLE GIRL NEEDS A LOVING HOME. VERY RICH PARENTS PREFERRED, AS LITTLE TRACY NEEDS LOTS OF TOYS, PRESENTS AND PETS TO MAKE UP FOR HER TRAGIC PAST.

Elaine is useless. Doesn't have a clue. She didn't even let me get specially kitted out for the photograph.

'We want you looking natural, Tracy,' she said.

Well I turned out looking too flipping natural. Hair all over the place and a scowl on my face because that stupid photographer kept treating me like a baby, telling me to Watch the Birdie. And the things Elaine wrote about me!

TRACY

Tracy is a lively, healthy, chatty, ten-year-old who has been in care for a number of years. Consequently she has a few behaviour problems and needs firm loving handling in a long-term foster home.

I ask you!

'How could you *do* this to me, Elaine?' I shrieked when I saw it. 'Is that the best thing you can say about me? That I'm *healthy*? And anyway I'm not. What about my hay fever?'

'I also say you're lively. And chatty.'

'Yeah. Well, we all know what that means. Cheeky. Difficult. Bossy.'

'You said it, Tracy,' Elaine murmured.

'And all this guff about behaviour problems! What do I do, eh? I don't go round beating people up? Well, not many. And I don't smash the furniture. Hardly ever.'

'Tracy, it's very understandable that you have a few problems—'

'I *don't*! And then how could you ask for someone to handle me *firmly*?'

'And lovingly,' said Elaine. 'I put loving too.'

'Oh yes, they'll tell me how much they love me as they lay into me with a cane. Honestly, Elaine, you're round the twist. You're just going to attract a bunch of creepy child-beaters with this crummy advert.'

But it didn't even attract them. No-one replied at all.

Elaine kept telling me not to worry, as if it was somehow my fault. I know if she'd only get her act together and do a really flash advert there'd be heaps of offers. I bet.

But maybe I'm wasting my time nagging Elaine. This woman who's coming this afternoon might be just the chance I've been waiting for. If she's a real writer then she'll know how to jazz it all up so that I sound really fantastic. Only I've got to present myself to

her in a special way so that she'll pick me out from all the others and just do a feature on me. So what am I going to do, eh?

Aha!

Not aha. More like boo-hoo. Only I don't ever cry, of course.

I don't want to write down what happened. I don't think I want to be a writer any more.

I tried, I really did. I went flying up to my bedroom straight after lunch and I did my best to make myself look pretty. I know my hair is untidy so I tried scragging it back into these little sticky-out plaits. Camilla had little plaits and everyone cooed over them and said how cute she looked. I thought my face looked a bit bare when I'd done the plaits so I wetted some of the side bits with spit and tried to make them go into curls.

I still looked a bit boring so I decided to liven my face up a bit. So I sneaked round to Adele's room. She's sixteen and she's got a Saturday job in BHS and she's got a drawer absolutely chock-a-block with make-up. I borrowed a bit of blusher to give myself some colour in my cheeks. And then I thought I'd try out a pink glossy lipstick too. And mascara to make my eyelashes look long. I tried a bit on my eyebrows too, to make them stand out. And I put a lot of powder on to be

like the icing on a cake. I thought I looked OK when I'd finished. Well, at least I looked different.

I changed my clothes too. I didn't want this writer to see me in a scrubby old T-shirt and skirt. No way. It had to be posh frock time. Only I don't really have a posh frock of my own. I did try on a few of Adele's things but somehow they didn't really suit me.

So then I started thinking about all the other girls. Louise had this really fantastic frock that she got a couple of years ago from some auntie. A real posh party frock with smocking and a flouncy skirt and its own sewn-in frilly white petticoat. It was a bit small for her now, of course, but she could just about squeeze into it for special days. And Louise and I are about the same size.

I knew Louise would go spare if she saw me parading around in her best party frock but I decided it might be worth it if I made a great impression on the writer woman first. So I beetled along the corridor towards her room, but I didn't have any luck. Louise was in her room. With Justine. I heard their voices.

They were discussing me, actually. And nappies. They were snorting with laughter and normally I'd have marched right in and punched their silly smirky faces but I knew if I got into a fight Jenny would send me to my room and make me stay there and I'd miss out on meeting the woman writer.

So with *extreme* self-control I walked away, still musing on what I was going to wear. I

know it's summer, but I'd started to feel a bit shaky and shivery so I put on this mohair sweater that Julie knitted me for Christmas. When Julie and Ted dumped me I vowed not to have anything to do with them and I even thought about cutting up the mohair sweater into little woolly hankies but I couldn't quite do it. It's a pretty fantastic sweater actually, with the name Tracy in bright blue letters. That way it's obvious it's mine, specially made for me. Of course it's a bit tickly and prickly, but my mum once said you have to suffer if you want to look beautiful.

She's always looked beautiful. I don't half wish I took after her. I wasn't too bad as a baby. I was still quite cute as a toddler. But then I went off in a big way.

Still, I was trying my hardest to look OK. I only had my old skirt to wear with my mohair sweater, and there were dark blue stains all down one side where a biro exploded in my pocket, but I couldn't help that. The woman writer might just think it was a tie-and-dye effect. And at least the blue matched the lettering on my jumper.

I kept on prinking and preening in my room. I heard all the other kids go clattering downstairs. I heard Louise and Justine go giggle-snigger-titter along the corridor. My face started burning so that I didn't need my blusher. Then I heard Adele rampaging around because some rotten so-and-so had been in her room and rifled through all her make-up and mucked it all up. I decided to hang about in my room a bit longer.

I heard the front door bell. I heard Jenny talking to someone down in the hall. I heard them go into the sitting-room. I knew it was time to make my Entrance.

So I went running down the stairs and barging into the sitting-room with this great big smile on my face. It's no use looking sad or sulky if you want people to like you. Mum always tells me to give her a big smile. Even when she's saying goodbye to me. You can't look gloomy or it just upsets people and they don't want any more to do with you.

You've got to have this great big s-s-s-m-m-m-i-i-i-l-l-l-e-e-e.

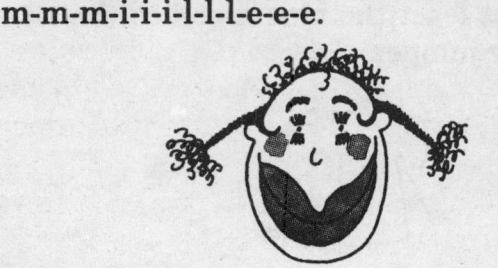

Everyone looked up at me when I went into the sitting-room. And they all smiled too. Just for a moment I was daft enough to think they were all smiling back at me. But then I saw they were the wrong sort of smiles. They were smirks. And Justine and Louise nudged each other and giggled and spluttered and whooped. And Adele glared at me. Peter Ingham was the only one with a proper smile. He came over to me. He was blinking a bit rapidly.

'You look . . . nice, Tracy,' he said.

But I knew he was lying. It was no use kidding myself. It was obvious I looked a right prat. Jenny's pretty laid back about appearances but even she looked shocked at the sight of me. And it looked like all that effort was for nothing, because she didn't seem to have the woman writer person with her after all.

I've seen women writers on chat shows on the telly. They're quite glamorous, like film stars, with glittery frocks and high heels and lots of jewellery. They look a bit like my mum, only nowhere near as pretty of course.

The woman with Jenny looked like some boring social worker or teacher. Scruffy brown hair. No make-up. Scrubby T-shirt and rumpled jeans. A bit like me on an off-day, grown up.

69

I decided to slope off back to my bedroom. It seemed sensible to steer clear of Adele anyway. But Jenny caught hold of me by the back of my jumper.

'Hang about, Tracy. I thought you wanted to meet Cam Lawson.'

'Who?' I said.

'You know. The writer. I told you,' Jenny hissed. Then she lowered her voice even more. 'Why are you wearing your winter jumper when it's boiling hot today? And what on earth have you done to your face?'

'She thinks she looks pretty,' said Justine, and she clutched Louise and they both shrieked.

'Pipe down, you two,' said Jenny. 'Tracy. Tracy!' She hung on to me firmly, stopping me barging over to that stupid pair of titterers so as I could bang their heads together. 'Leave them, Tracy. Come and meet Cam.'

I wanted to meet this Cam (what sort of a silly name is that?) even though she didn't look a bit like a *proper* writer, but I sort of hung back. I'm usually the last person to feel shy, but somehow I suddenly didn't know what to say or what to do. So I growled something at Jenny and twisted away from her and stood in a corner by myself, just watching.

Peter came trotting after me. Justine and Louise were still having hysterics at my appearance. You could tell they'd actually got over the giggles by this time, but Justine kept going into further false whoops and Louise was almost as bad.

'Don't take any notice of them,' Peter whispered.

'I don't,' I said crossly.

'I like your jumper,' said Peter. 'And your make-up. And the new hairstyle.'

'Then you're mad. It looks a mess. I look a mess. I look a mess *on purpose*,' I said fiercely. 'So you needn't feel sorry for me, Peter Ingham. You just clear off and leave me alone, right?'

Peter fidgeted from one foot to the other, looking worried.

'Clear off, you stupid little creep,' I said.

So of course he did clear off then. I wondered why I'd said it. OK, he *is* a creep, but he's not really that bad. I'd said he could be my friend. And it was a lot better when he was with me than standing all by myself, watching everyone over the other side of the room clustered round this Cam person calling herself a writer.

She's a weird sort of woman if you ask me. She was chatting away and yet you could tell she was really nervous inside. She

kept fidgeting with her pen and notebook and I was amazed to see she bites her nails! She's a great big grown-up woman and yet she does a dopey kid's thing like that. Well, she's not great big, she's little and skinny, but even so!

My mum has the most beautiful finger-nails, very long and pointy and polished. She varnishes them every day. I just love that smell of nail varnish, that sharp peardrop niff that makes your nostrils twitch. Jenny caught me happily sniffing nail varnish one day, and do you know what she thought? Only that I was inhaling it, like glue sniffing. Did you ever? I let her think it too. *I* wasn't going to tell her I just liked the smell because it reminds me of Mum.

I'll tell you another weird thing about Cam Whatsit. She sat on one of our rickety old chairs, her legs all draped round the rungs, and she talked *to* the children. Most adults that come here talk *at* children.

They tell you what to do.

They go on and on about themselves.

They talk about you.

They ask endless stupid questions.

They make personal comments.

Even the social workers are at it. Or they strike this special nothing-you-can-say-would-shock-me-sweetie pose and they make stupid statements.

'I guess you're feeling really angry and upset today, Tracy,' they twitter, when I've wrecked my bedroom or got into a fight or shouted and sworn at someone, so that it's *obvious* I'm angry and upset.

They do this to show me that they understand. Only they don't understand peanuts. *They're* not the ones in care. I am.

I thought Cam Thing would ask questions and take down case histories in her notebook, all brisk and organized. But from what I could make out over in the corner she had a very different way of doing things.

She smiled a bit and fidgeted a lot and sort of weighed everybody up, and they all had a good stare at her. Two of the little kids

tried to climb up on to her lap because they do
that to anyone who sits down. It's not because
they *like* the person, it's just they like being
cuddled. They'd cry to have a cuddle with a
cross-eyed gorilla, I'm telling you.

Most strangers to children's homes get all
flattered and make a great fuss of the littlies
and come on like Mary Poppins. This Cam
seemed a bit surprised, even a bit put out.
I don't blame her. Little Wayne in particular
has got the runniest nose of all time and he
likes to bury his head affectionately into your
chest, wiping it all down your front.

Cam held him at arm's length, and when
he tried his burrowing trick she distracted
him by giving him her pen. He liked flicking
the catch up and down.

She let little Becky have a ride on her
foot at the same time, so she didn't feel left
out and bawl. Becky kept trying to climb up
her leg, pulling her jeans up. Some of Cam's leg
got exposed. It was a pretty ropey sort of leg if
you ask me. A bit hairy for a start. My mum
always shaves her legs, and she wears sheer
see-through tights to show them off. This
Cam had socks like a schoolgirl. Only they
were quite funny brightly patterned socks.
I thought the red and yellow bits were just
squares at first, but then I got a bit closer and
saw they were books. I wouldn't mind having

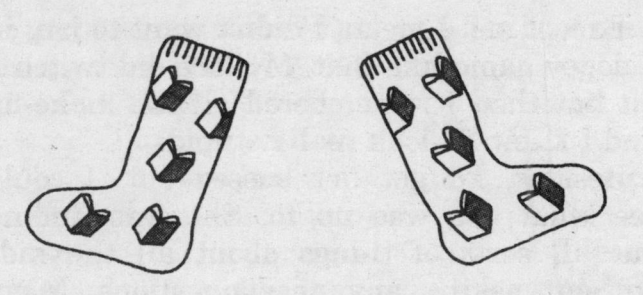

a pair of socks like that myself, if I'm going to write all these books.

She's written books. Old Cammy. Cammy-knicker, ha-ha. The other kids asked her and she told them. She said she wrote some stories but they didn't sell much so she also wrote some romantic stuff. She doesn't look the romantic type to me.

Adele got interested then because she loves all those soppy love books and Cam told her some titles and the boys all tittered and went yuck yuck and Jenny got a bit narked but Cam said she didn't mind, they were mostly yuck but she couldn't help it if that's what people liked to read.

Then they all started talking about reading. Maxy said he liked this book *Where the Wild Things Are* because the boy in that is called Max, and Cam said she knew that book and she made a Wild Thing face and then everyone else did too.

Except me. I mean, I didn't want to join in a dopey game like that. My face did twitch a bit but then I remembered all the make-up and I knew I'd look really stupid.

Besides, I'd got her sussed out. I could see what she was up to. She was finding out all sorts of things about all the kids without asking any nosy questions. Maxy went on about his dad being a Wild Thing. Adele went on about love, only of course real life wasn't like that, and love didn't ever last and people split up and sometimes didn't even go on loving their children.

Even little creepy Peter piped up about these Catherine Cookson books that his nan used to like, and he told Cam how he used to read them to her because her eyes had gone all blurry. And then *his* eyes went a bit blurry too, remembering his nan, and Cam's hand reached out sort of awkwardly. She didn't quite manage to hold his hand, she just sort of tapped his bony wrist sympathetically.

'My nan's dead too. And my mum. They're both together in heaven now. Angels, like,' said Louise, lisping a bit.

She always does that. Puts on this sweet little baby act when there are grown-ups about. Like she was a little angel herself. Ha. Our little Louise can be even worse than me when she wants. She's had three foster

placements, no, was it four? Anyway, none of them worked out. But Louise always swore she didn't care. We used to have this pact that we'd do our best not to get fostered at all and we'd stay together at the Home till we got to be eighteen and then we'd get them to house us together. In our own modern flat. We'd got it all planned out. Louise even started thinking about our furniture, the ornaments, the posters on the walls.

And then Justine came and everything was spoilt. Oh how I hate that Justine Littlewood. I'm glad I broke her silly Mickey Mouse alarm clock. I'd like to break her into little bits and all.

Anyway, Louise lisped on about angels and I'll give that Cam her due, she didn't go all simpering and sentimental and pat Louise on her curly head and talk about the little darling. She stayed calm and matter-of-fact, and started talking about angels and wondering what they would look like.

'That's simple, Miss. They've got these big wings and long white nighties and those gold plate things stuck on the back of their heads,' said Justine.

'Draw one for me,' said Cam, offering her pen and notebook.

'OK,' said Justine, though she can't draw for toffee. Then she had a close look at the

77

pen in her hand. 'Here, it's a Mickey Mouse pen. Look, Louise, see the little Mickey. Oh Miss, where did you get this pen? It's great! I love Mickey, I do. I've got this Mickey Mouse alarm clock, my dad gave it me, only some *pig* broke it deliberately.' Justine looked over her shoulder and glared at me.

I glared back, making out I couldn't care less. And I *couldn't*. My face started burning, but that was just because of my mohair sweater.

Justine drew her stupid angel and Cam nodded at it.

'Yes, that's the way people usually draw angels.' She looked at Louise. 'So is this the way you imagine your mum and your nan?'

'Well. Sort of,' said Louise.

'Is that the sort of nightie that your nan would wear? And what about the halo, the gold plate bit. Would that fit neatly on top of her hairstyle?'

Louise giggled uncertainly, not sure what she was getting at.

'You draw me what you think your mum and nan look like as angels,' said Cam.

Louise started, but she can't draw much either, and she kept scribbling over what she'd done.

'This is silly,' she said, giving up.

I knew what Cam was on about. I'd have

done a really great drawing of Louise's mum and nan in natty angel outfits. Like this.

'I'll draw you an angel, Miss,' said Maxy, grabbing at the pen. 'I'll draw me as an angel and I'll have big wings so I can fly like an aeroplane, y-e-e-e-o-o-o-w, y-e-e-e-o-o-o-w.' He went on making his dopey aeroplane noises all the time he was drawing.

Then the others had a go, even the big ones. I got a bit nearer and craned my neck to see what they'd all drawn. I didn't think any of them very inspired.

I knew exactly what I'd draw if she asked me. It wouldn't be a silly old angel.

Then Cam looked up. She caught my eye. She did ask me.

'Have a go?' she said, dead casual.

I gave this little shrug as if I couldn't care less. Then I sauntered forward, very slowly. I held out my hand for the pen.

'This is Tracy,' said Jenny, poking her big nose in. 'She's the one who wants to be a writer.'

I felt my face start burning again.

'What, her?' said Justine. 'You've got to be joking.'

'Now Justine,' said Jenny. 'Tracy's written heaps and heaps in her Life Book.'

'Yeah, but it's all rubbish,' said Justine, and her hand shot out and she made a grab

underneath my jumper, where I was keeping this book for safety. I bashed out at her but I wasn't quick enough. She snatched the book from me before I could stop her.

'Give that here!' I shrieked.

'It's rubbish, I tell you, listen,' said Justine, and she opened my book and started reading in a silly high-pitched baby voice "Once upon a time there was a little girl called Tracy Beaker and that sounds stupid and no wonder because I *am* stupid and I wet the bed and— Ooooowwww!" '

Things got a bit hazy after that. But I got my book back. And Justine's nose became a wonderful scarlet fountain. I was glad glad glad. I wanted her whole body to spout blood but Jenny had hold of me by this time and she was shouting for Mike and I got hauled off to the Quiet Room. Only I wasn't quiet in there. I yelled my head off. I went on yelling when Jenny came to try and calm me down. And then Jenny went away and someone else came into the room. I wasn't sure who it was at first because when I yell my eyes screw up and I can't see properly. Then I made out the jeans and the T-shirt and the shock of hair and I knew it was Cam Whosit and that made me burn all over until I felt like a junior Joan of Arc.

There was me, throwing a hairy fit, and there was her standing there watching me. I don't care about people like Jenny or Elaine seeing me. They're used to it. Nearly all children in care have a roaring session once in a while. I have them more than once, actually. And I usually just let rip, but now I felt like a right raving loony in front of her.

But I didn't stop yelling all the same. There was no point. She'd already seen me at it. And heard me too. She didn't try to stop me. She wasn't saying a word. She was standing there. And she had this awful expression on her face. I couldn't stand it. She looked sorry for me.

I wasn't having that. So I told her to go away. That's putting it politely. I yelled some very rude words at her. And she just sort of shrugged and nodded and went off.

I was left screaming and swearing away, all by myself.

But I'm OK now. I'm not in the Quiet Room any more. I stayed in there ever such a long time and I even had my tea in there on a tray but now I'm in my bedroom and I've been writing and writing and writing away and it looks like I can't *help* being a writer. I've written so much I've got a big lump on the longest finger of my right hand. You look.

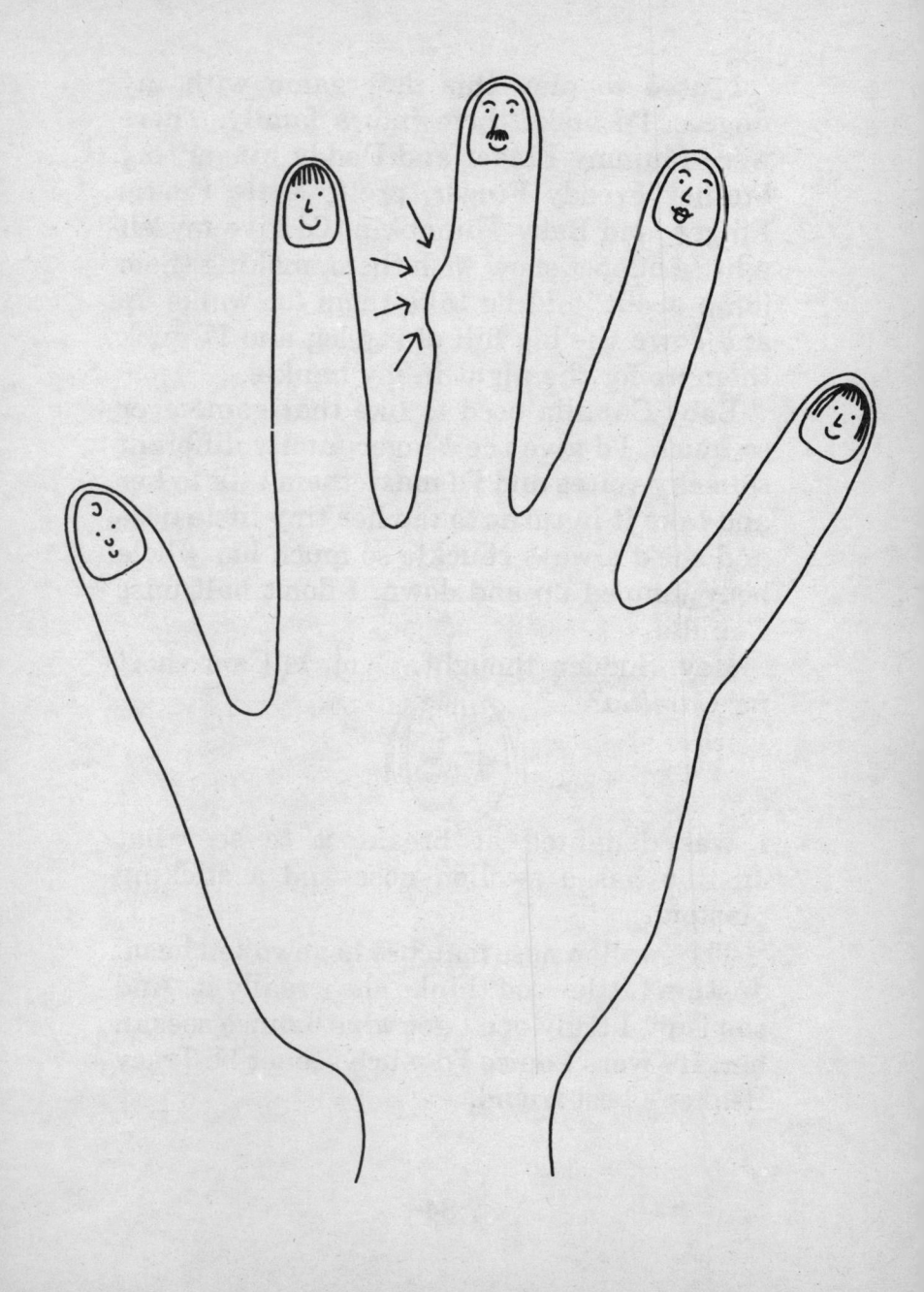

I used to play this daft game with my fingers. I'd make them into a family. There were Mummy Finger and Daddy Finger, big brother Freddy Finger, pretty little Pinkie Finger, and Baby Thumbkin. I'd give myself a little puppet show with them, making them jump about, and I'd take them for walks up and down the big hill of my leg and I'd tuck them up for the night in my hankie.

Baby Camilla used to like that game ever so much. I'd give the Finger family different squeaky voices and I'd make them talk to her and take it in turns to tap her tiny little nose and she'd always chuckle so much her whole body jumped up and down. I don't half miss Camilla.

Hey. Sudden thought. Cam. Is Cam short for *Camilla*?

I was delighted at breakfast to see that Justine has a swollen nose and a sticking plaster.

The swollen nose matches her swollen head. Justine Littlewood thinks she's really it. And she isn't. I truly don't get what Louise sees in her. If *I* were Louise I'd much sooner be Tracy Beaker's best friend.

What really gets me is that I was the one who palled up with Justine first. She turned up at the Home one evening, all down and droopy because her mum had cleared off with some bloke and left Justine and her two little brothers and her dad to get on with it. Only her dad couldn't get on with it, and the kids got taken into care. The brothers got into a short-term foster home because they were still nearly at the baby stage and not too much bother. But Justine didn't get taken on too, because they thought she'd be difficult.

I generally like kids who are difficult. And I thought I liked the look of Justine. And the sound of her. Because after the first droopy evening she suddenly found her tongue and she started sounding off at everyone, getting really stroppy and swearing. She knew even more swear words than I do.

She was like that all week but she shut up on Sunday. Her dad was supposed to see her on Sunday. She was sitting waiting for him right after breakfast, though he wasn't supposed to be coming till eleven o'clock. Eleven came and went. And twelve. And then it was dinnertime and Justine wouldn't eat her chicken. She sat at the window all afternoon, not budging.

My tummy went tight whenever I looked at her. I knew what it was like. I used to sit like that. Not just here. I used to wait at both my crummy foster homes. And the children's homes in between. Waiting for my mum to come.

But now I've got myself sorted out. No more dumb sitting about for me. Because my mum's probably too far away to come on a quick visit. Yeah, that's it, she's probably abroad somewhere, she's always fancied travelling.

She's maybe in France.

Or Spain, she likes sunshine.

What am I thinking of? She'll have gone to the States. Maybe Hollywood. My mum looks so great she'd easily get into the movies.

You can't hop on a bus and visit your daughter when you're hundreds and thousands of miles away in Hollywood, now can you?

All the same, even though I don't sit waiting, I always go a bit tingly when there's a
knock at the door. I hold my breath, waiting
to see who it is, just in case . . .

So I could understand what old Justine
was going through. I didn't try to talk to
her because I knew she'd snap my head off,
but I sort of sidled up to her and dropped a
lollipop on her lap and backed away. It wasn't
exactly my lollipop. I'd snaffled several from
little Wayne. His dopey mum is younger than
Adele and she hasn't got a clue about babies.
Whenever she comes she brings Wayne lollipops. Well, they've got sticks, haven't they?
We don't want little Wayne giving himself a
poke in the eye. And he's normally so drooly
that if you add a lot of lolly-lick as well he
gets stickier than Superglue. So it's really a
kindness to nick his lollies when he's not
looking.

'But why did you want to give one to
that Justine?' Louise asked. 'She's horrible,
Tracy. She barged right into me on the stairs
yesterday and she didn't even say sorry, she
just called me a very rude word indeed.' Louise
whispered it primly.

'Um. Did she really say that?' I said, giggling. 'Oh she's not so bad really. And anyway,
I didn't give her the *red* lollipop. I saved that
for you.'

'Thanks, Trace,' said Louise, and she beamed at me.

Oh we were like *that* in those days.

I kept an eye on Justine. She didn't budge for a good half hour, letting the lollipop lie in her lap. And then I saw her hand creep out. She unwrapped it and gave it one small suspicious lick, as if I'd poisoned it. But it must have tasted OK because she took another lick, and then another, and then she settled down for a good long suck. Lollipops can be very soothing to the stomach.

She didn't say thank you or anything. And when she eventually had to give up waiting and go to bed she stalked off by herself. But the next day at breakfast she gave me this little nod. So I nodded back and flicked a cornflake in her direction and she flicked one back, and we ended up having this good game

of tiddlyflakes and after that we were friends. Not best friends. Louise was my best friend. Ha.

She moaned at first.

'Why do we have to have that Justine hanging round us all the time?' she complained. 'I don't like her, Trace. She's dead tough.'

'Well, I want to be tough too. You've got to be tough. What do you mean, *I'm* tougher than Justine,' I said, sticking my chin out.

'Nutter,' said Louise.

It started to get to me though. I started swearing worse than Justine and Jenny got really mad at me because Maxy started copying me and even little Wayne would come out with a right mouthful when he felt like it.

So then I started the Dare Game. I've always won any dare. Until Justine came along.

I dared her to say the rudest word she could think of when the vicar came on a visit. And she did.

She dared me to go out in the garden stark naked. And I did.

I dared her to eat a worm. And she did.

She dared *me* to eat a worm.

I said that wasn't fair. She couldn't copy my dare. Louise opened her big mouth and said that I hated worms. 'Then I dare her to eat *two* worms,' said Justine. So I did.

I *did*. Sort of. It wasn't my fault they made me sick. I did swallow them first. Justine said I just spat them out straight away but I *didn't*.

I thought hard. I happen to be a crack hand at skateboarding. Justine's not much good at getting her balance and her steering's rotten. So I fixed up this skateboard assault course round the garden, with sloping benches and all sorts. And I dared Justine to have a go. So she did.

She fell over a lot. But she kept getting up and carrying on. So I said she was disqualified. But Louise said Justine should still win the bet if she completed the course. And she did.

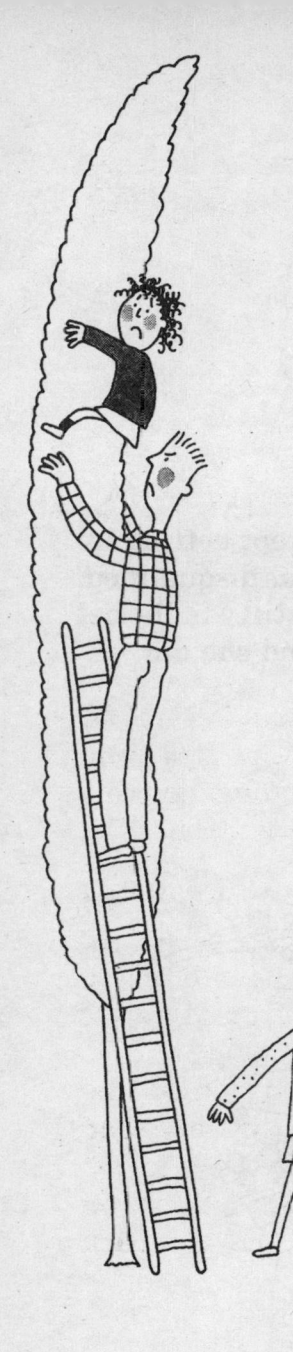

Then Justine dared me
to climb the tree
at the end of the garden.
So I did.
It wasn't *my* fault
I didn't get right to
the top. I didn't ask
that stupid Mike to
interfere. But Justine said
I'd lost that dare,
and Louise backed her up.
I couldn't believe my ears.
Louise was *my* friend.

We couldn't do any more dares because Jenny PUT HER FOOT DOWN. You don't argue when she does that.

The next day Justine's famous dad put in an appearance at long last. Justine had gone on and on about how good-looking he was, just like a pop star, and he actually had an evening job singing in pubs, which was why he couldn't be at home to look after her and her brothers. Well, you should have seen him. Starting to go bald. Pot belly. Medallion. He wasn't *quite* wearing a frilly shirt and flares, but almost.

You wouldn't catch me wanting a dad like that. But Justine gave a weird little whoop when she saw him and jumped up into his arms like a great big baby. He took her on some dumb outing and when she got back

she was all bubbly and bouncy and showing off this . . . this present he'd bought her.

← whoops!

I don't know why, but I felt really narked at Justine. It was all right when she didn't get a visit, like us lot. But now I kept picking on her and saying silly sniggery things about her dad. And then she burst into tears.

I was a bit shocked. I didn't say anything *that* bad. And I never thought a really tough girl like Justine would ever cry. *I* don't ever cry, no matter what. I mean, my mum hasn't managed to come and visit me for donkey's years and I don't even *have* a dad, but catch me crying.

And then I got another shock. Because Louise turned on me.

'You are horrid, Tracy,' she said. And then she put her arms right round Justine and gave her a big hug. 'Don't take any notice of her. She's just jealous.'

Me, jealous? Of Justine? Of Justine's dopey dumb dad? She had to be joking.

But it didn't look like she was joking. She and Justine went off together, their arms round each other.

I told myself I didn't care. Although I did care a little bit then. And I did wonder if I'd gone over the top with my remarks. I can have a very cutting tongue.

I thought I'd smooth things over at breakfast. Maybe even tell Justine I hadn't really meant any of it. Not actually apologize, of course, but show her that I was sorry. But it was too late. I was left on my own at breakfast. Louise didn't sit next to me in her usual seat. She went and sat at the table by the window – with Justine.

'Hey, Louise,' I called. And then I called again, louder. 'Have you gone deaf or something?' I yelled.

But she could hear me all right. She just wasn't talking to me. She wasn't my best friend any more. She was Justine's.

All I've got is silly squitty twitty Peter Ingham. Oh, maybe he's not so bad. I was writing all this down when there was this tiny tapping at my door. As if some timid little insect was scrabbling away out there. I told this beetle to buzz off because I was busy, but it went on scribble-scrabbling. So eventually I heaved myself off my bed and went to see what it wanted.

'Do you want to play, Tracy?' he said.

'Play?' I said witheringly. 'What do you think I am, Peter Ingham? Some kind of infant? I'm busy writing.' But I'd been writing

so much my whole arm ached and my writing lump was all red and throbbing. Oh, how we writers suffer for our art! It's chronic, it really is.

So I did just wonder if it was time for a little diversion.

'What sort of games do *you* play then, little Peetle-Beetle?'

He blinked a bit and shuffled backwards as if I was about to squash him, but he managed to squeak out something about paper games.

'Paper games?' I said. 'Oh, I see. Do we make a football out of paper and then give it a kick so that it blows away? What fun. Or do we make a dear little teddy out of paper and give it a big hug and squash it flat? Even better.'

Peter giggled nervously. 'No, Tracy, pen and paper games. I always used to play noughts and crosses with my nan.'

'Oh gosh, how incredibly thrilling,' I said.

Beetles don't understand sarcasm.

'Good, *I* like noughts and crosses too,' he said, producing a pencil out of his pocket.

There was no deterring him. So we played paper games after that.

I suppose it passed the time a bit. And now I've just spotted something. Right at the bottom of the page, in teeny tiny beetle writing, there's a little message.

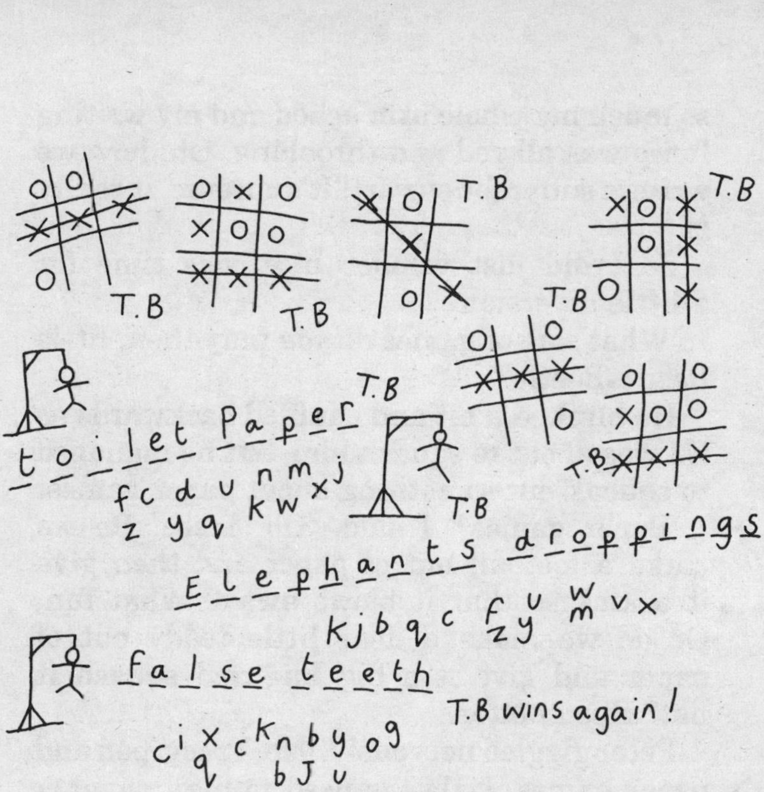

toilet paper

f c d u n m j
z y q k w x

Elephants droppings

k j b q c f u w v x
z y m

false teeth

T.B wins again!

c i x c k n b y o g
q b J u

Justine Littlewood's father
met my nan
At the sewage works
he said to her

CENSORED!

I don't half like
you, Tracy.
signed Peter Ingham.

Guess what! I've got a letter!

Not another soppy little message from Peter. A real private letter that came in the post, addressed to Ms Tracy Beaker.

I haven't had many letters just recently. Oh, there have been plenty of letters *about* me. Elaine's got a whole library of files on me. I've had a secret rifle through them and you should just see some of the mean horrid things they say about me. I had a good mind to sue them for libel. Yeah, that would be great. And I'd get awarded all these damages, hundreds of thousands of pounds, and I'd be able to thumb my nose at Justine and Jenny and Elaine and all the others. I'd just clutch my lovely lolly in my hot little hand and go off and . . .

Well, I'd have my own house, right? And I'd employ someone to foster me. But because I'd be paying them, *they'd* have to do everything *I* said. I'd order them to make me a whole birthday cake to myself every single day of the week and they'd just have to jump to it and do so.

I wouldn't let anybody else in to share it with me.

Not even Peter. I had to share my *real* birthday cake with him. And he gave me a nudge and said 'What's the matter, Tracy? Don't you feel well?' just when I'd closed my

eyes tight and was in the middle of making my birthday wish. So it got all muddled and I lost my thread and now if my mum doesn't come for me it's all that Peter Ingham's fault.

Well, maybe it is.

But I'd still let him come round to my house sometimes and we could play paper games. They're quite good fun really, because I always win.

Who else could I have in my house? I could try and get Camilla. I'd look after her. I could get a special playpen and lots of toys. I've always liked the look of all that baby junk. I don't suppose I had much of that sort of thing when I was a baby. Yeah, I could

have a proper nursery in my house and when Camilla wasn't using it I could muck about in there, just for a laugh.

I wonder if Camilla remembers me now? That's the trouble with babies.

I wonder if Cam *is* short for Camilla? That's who my letter was from.

I was a bit disappointed at first. I thought it was from my mum. I know she's never written to me before but still, when Jenny handed it to me at breakfast I just clutched at the envelope and held it tight and shut my eyes quick because they got suddenly hot and prickly and if I was a snively sort of person I might well have cried.

'What's up with Tracy?' the other kids mumbled.

I gave a great swallow and sniff and opened my eyes and said, 'Nothing's up! Look, I've got a letter! A letter from—'

'I think it's maybe from Cam Lawson,' Jenny said, very quickly indeed.

I caught my breath. 'Yeah. Cam Lawson. See that? She's written me my own personal letter. And she's not written to any of you lot. See! She's written to *me*.'

'So what does she say then?'

'Never you mind. It's *private*.'

I went off to read it all by myself. I didn't get around to it for a bit. I was thinking all these dopey things about my mum. And I had a bad attack of hay fever. And I didn't really want to read what Cam Lawson had to say anyway. She saw me having my hairy fit. I was scared she'd think me some sort of loony.

Only the letter was OK.

10 Beech Road
Kingtown

Dear Tracy

We didn't really get together properly when
I came on my visit. It was a pity because Jenny
told me a bit about you and I liked the sound of
you. She said you're very naughty and you like
writing.

I'm exactly the opposite. I've
always been very very good. Especially
when I was at school. You wouldn't half
have teased me.

I'm not quite so good now, thank goodness.

And I hate writing. Because it's what I do
for a living and every day I get up from my cornflakes
and go and sit at my typewriter and my hands clench
into fists and I go cross-eyed staring at the blank
paper - and I think - what a stupid way to earn a
living. Why don't I do something else? Only I'm
useless at everything else so I just have to carry
on with my writing.

Are you carrying on with your writing? You're
telling your own story? An actual autobiography?
Most girls your age wouldn't have much
to write about, but you're lucky in that
respect because so many different things
have happened to you.

Good luck with it.

Yours,

Cam

Lee Road Dumping
Ground for Difficult Kids

Dear Ms Lawson,
          Jenny says that's what I should
call you, Ms Lawson, although you wrote Cam
at the bottom of your letter. What sort of name is
Cam? If you're called Camilla then I think that's
a lovely name and don't see why you want to muck
it up. I had a friend in this other home called
Camilla and she liked her name. I had a special way
of saying it, Ca-miiii-lla, and she'd always
giggle. She was only a baby but very bright.
          Why don't you mind me being naughty?
Actually, its not always my fault that I get
into trouble. People just pick on me. Lots of
people, but I won't name names because I don't
tell tales, not like some people.

Do you like my drawing? I
liked yours, I thought they
were funny. What do you
mean, you hate writing?

Tracy Beaker did this.
Tracy Beaker did that.
Um Tracy Beaker is
awful!

GLUE

I think that's weird when it's what you do. I like writing. I think it's ever so easy. I just start and it goes on and on. The only trouble is that it hurts your hand and you get a big lump on your finger. And ink all over your hand and clothes and paper if some clueless toddler has been chewing on your felt tip.

Are you having trouble writing your article about us? I could help you if you liked. I can tell you anything you need to know about me. And the others. How about it?

Yes I am still writing my autobiography. I like that word. I asked Jenny and she said it's a story about yourself, and that's right, that's exactly what I'm writing. I'd let you have a look at it but it's strictly personal. Don't take any notice of what that moron Justine read out. There are some really good bits, honest.

Yours
From your fellow writer

Tracy Beaker

R.S.V.P

That means you've got to reply.

10 Beech Road.

Dear Tracy,

Thanks for your lovely letter. It made me laugh. Do you know what? I think you're a born writer.

I could do with some help on my feature. Are you around next Saturday morning? Hope to see you then. Cam.

I hate Camilla. I used to get teased rotten at school for having such a soppy name.

Dear Camilla,

It's not a soppy name. You've got to be proud of it. You want to try having a name like Tracy Beaker. Excuse this crummy writing paper. Jenny lent me the first lot but she says I'm costing her a small fortune in paper and can't I give it a rest. So I borrowed this from one of the little ones. Isn't it yucky? I know.

← This is Goblinda the Goblin and she's going to gob all over these daft fairies.

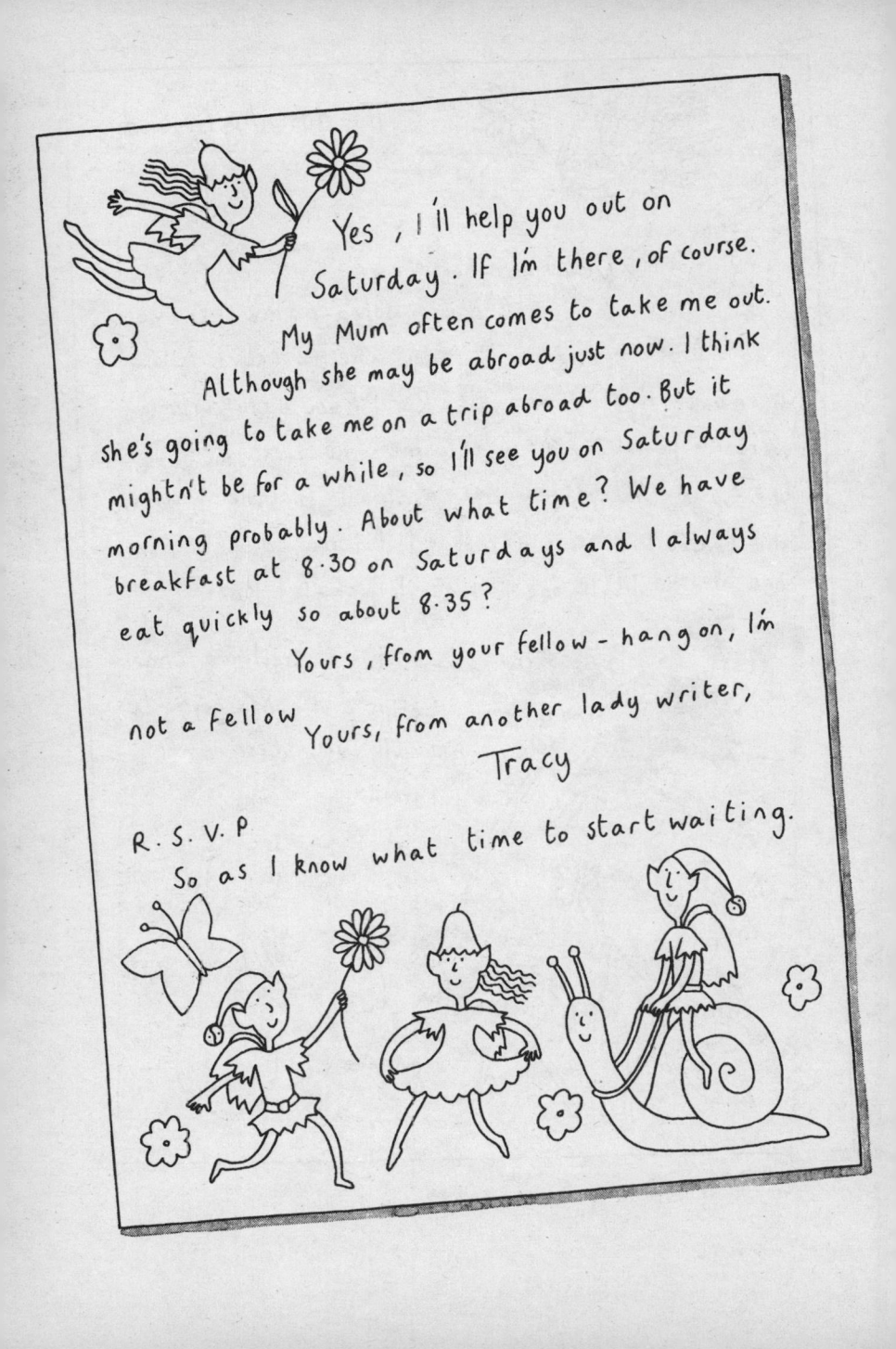

Yes, I'll help you out on Saturday. If I'm there, of course.

My Mum often comes to take me out. Although she may be abroad just now. I think she's going to take me on a trip abroad too. But it mightn't be for a while, so I'll see you on Saturday morning probably. About what time? We have breakfast at 8.30 on Saturdays and I always eat quickly so about 8.35?

Yours, from your fellow - hang on, I'm not a fellow

Yours, from another lady writer,

Tracy

R.S.V.P
So as I know what time to start waiting.

10 Beech Road

Dear Sister Writer,

See you Saturday morning. 8·35 impossible.

I look like this at 8·35.

zzzz

How about 10·35?

Cam. Sorry. Camilla. Ugh!

P.S. I love Goblinda. Put her in a story.

Imagine staying in your bed half the morning. She is lazy. And she was late even then. It was 10.41 before she turned up. I'd practically given her up. She's supposed to be a professional writer and yet she can't even keep an appointment on time.

She's pretty hopeless if you ask me. She didn't half muck up this morning. I'd got it all worked out. I was ready to fill her in on all the facts. Mostly about me, of course. But I thought maybe she might fancy interviewing Peter too, to balance things up. A girl's point of view, and a boy's. No need to bother with any of the others.

Cam's got this dinky little tape recorder and after just one minute of instruction I mastered all the mechanism and had great fun fast-forwarding and rewinding and playing back. I had a little go first, trying out all my different accents, doing my Australian G'day routine and my American gangster and my special Donald Duck, but then I decided we'd better get down to business and as I'm not the sort of girl to hog the limelight I said Peter could go first.

He backed away from the tape recorder as if it was a loaded gun.

'Don't be so silly, Peter. Just act normal and speak into it.'

'What shall I say?' Peter squeaked.

I sighed impatiently. 'Just tell Cam your life story.'

'But I haven't got a story. I couldn't think of anything to put when Elaine gave me that book,' said Peter. 'I lived with my nan. And she died. So I came here. That's all there is.'

'That's OK, Peter. Don't let Tracy bully you into it. You don't have to say anything,' said Cam.

'What a cheek! I'm not a bully. Huh, *I* was the kid who always *got* bullied. This other Home I was in, there was this huge great teenage bloke, and he was a really tough skinhead and he had these bovver boots and I filled them up with custard for a joke and he didn't see the funny side of it

and yet he didn't half look hilarious, all this frothy yellow liquid squishing up his trouser legs – so anyway, from then on my name was mud, and he really had it in for me. The things he used to do!'

I was about to launch into a long account but typical typical that Justine Littlewood came barging over.

'It's not fair, Miss. You're letting that stupid Tracy show off like mad, and you're not giving any of us a go.'

'You shut your face, blabbermouth,' I said. 'She's not come to see you lot. She's come to see *me*. A strictly private appointment. So clear off. Isn't that right, Cam?'

'Well. Yes, I've come to talk to you, Tracy. But we could all have a go on the tape recorder for a bit,' she said.

What a gutless creep she is. She was there just to see *me*. We had a proper business appointment. All she had to do was tell Justine and the others to buzz off. It wouldn't have mattered if Peter stayed, because he's not really any bother. But the others! It was useless. Practically the whole morning was wasted. She let them all muck around on the tape recorder and then some of the littlies wanted another go drawing with her Mickey Mouse pen, and then Jenny came

in with coffee for Cam and coke for us and it was like some big party. Only I didn't feel like the birthday girl. I felt squeezed out to the edge again.

After a bit I stomped off. I kept looking back over my shoulder and I thought she didn't even notice. But then she sidled up. She still had baby Becky on one hip and little Wayne clinging to her leg like a limpet. She gave me a dig in the back with her Mickey Mouse pen.

'Hey,' she said softly. 'Shall we get started on your interview now, Tracy?'

'Well, you've got all these other kids. Why waste your time with me?' I said acidly. 'I mean, I'm only the one you were *supposed* to see.'

'Tell you what. Let's go up to your room. Just you and me. How about it?'

'OK,' I said, yawning and shrugging. 'If you really want. I've gone off the idea now. But if you insist. Just for a minute or two.'

It took her a while to dump the baby and prise Wayne away, and then all the others kept clustering around, saying it wasn't fair. So do you know what she did? She said they could do interviews on her tape recorder. And she put *Justine* in charge of it.

'You aren't half making a mistake there, Cam. You're crazy. They'll wreck it in two minutes,' I said.

'No they won't. Justine will work it. And everyone take a two-minute turn. Introduce yourselves first, and then say whatever you want. But don't worry, Peter, you don't have to.'

'You are stark staring mad,' I said. 'Look, if anyone's in charge of that tape recorder it's got to be me. I'm the only one who knows how to work it properly.'

'Well, show Justine,' said Cam. 'Then she'll be able to work it too.'

'I'm not showing *her*,' I said. But in the end I did. And of course Justine was clueless and didn't catch on and I kept sighing and groaning and she got narked and gave me a push and I clenched my fist ready to give her a thump but Cam got in between us and said, 'Look, I'll run through it. Here's the record button, Justine, right?' and *eventually* Justine got the hang of it. I don't know why she's called Littlewood. Little*brain* would be far more appropriate.

Then Cam and I went up to my room and left them to it.

'You thought you'd found a way of getting Justine and me to make friends,' I said. 'But, ha-ha, it didn't work, did it? Because we're always going to be deadly enemies.'

Cam laughed at me. She laughed at the notice taped on my bedroom door too.

THIS ROOM BELONGS TO
TRACY BEAKER
STRICTLY PRIVATE
KEEP OUT ON PAIN OF DEATH.
AND IT WILL BE A VERY PAINFUL
DEATH TOO.

'It's OK. You can come in. You're my guest,' I said, opening the door for her.

My room looked a bit of a tip actually. I hadn't got round to making the bed and the floor was littered with socks and pyjama tops and bits of biscuit and pencil sharpenings, so she had to pick her way through. She didn't make a big thing of it though. She looked at all the stuff I've got pinned to my noticeboard, and she nodded a bit and smiled.

'Is that your mum?' Cam asked.

'Isn't she lovely? You'd really think she was a film star, wouldn't you? I think she maybe *is* a film star now. In Hollywood. And she'll be jetting over to see me soon. Maybe she'll take me back with her, and I'll get to be a film star too. A child star. The marvellous movie moppet, Tracy Beaker. Yeah. That would be great, eh?'

I spun around with a great grin, doing a cutsie-pie curtsey – and Cam caught on straight away and started clapping and acting like an adoring fan.

'I hope you're still going to be a writer too,' she said. 'Have you done any more about Goblinda?'

'Give us a chance. I've been too busy doing my autobiography,' I said.

'I suppose this autobiography of yours is strictly private?' Cam asked, sounding a bit wistful.

'Of course it is,' I said. But then I hesitated. Elaine the Pain has seen bits of it. And Louise and Littlebrain. And I did show a bit to Peter

actually, just to show him how much I'd done. So why shouldn't I show a bit to Cam too? As she's a sort of friend.

So I let her have a few peeps. I had to be a bit careful, because some of the stuff I've written about her isn't exactly flattering. She came across a description of her by accident, but she didn't take offence. She roared with laughter.

'You really should be the one writing this article about children in care, Tracy, not me. I think you'd make a far better job of it.'

'Yes, have you made a start on this article yet?'

She fidgeted a bit. 'Not really. It's difficult. You see, this magazine editor wants a very touching sentimental story about all these sad sweet vulnerable little children that will make her readers reach for a wad of Kleenex.'

'Yeah, that's the right approach.'

'Oh come off it, Tracy. None of you lot are at all *sweet*. You're all gutsy and stroppy and spirited. I want to write what you're really like but it won't be the sort of thing the editor wants.'

'And it won't be the sort of thing *I* want either. You've got to make me sound sweet, Cam! No-one will want me otherwise. I've gone past my sell-by date already. It gets

hopeless when you get older than five or six. You've stopped being a cute little toddler and started to be difficult. And I'm not pretty either so people won't take one look at my photo and start cooing. And then it's not like I'm up for adoption so people can't ever make me their little girl, not properly.'

'You're not up for adoption because you've still got your mum?'

'Exactly. And like I said, she'll be coming for me soon, but meanwhile I'd like to live in a proper homey home instead of this old dump. Otherwise I'll get institutionalized.'

Cam's eyebrows go up.

'I know what it means and all. I've heard Elaine and some of the other social workers going on about it. It's when you get so used to living in an institution like this that you never learn how to live in a proper home. And when you get to eighteen you can't cope and you don't know how to do your own shopping or cooking or anything. Although I can't see me ever having that problem. I bet I could cope right this minute living on my own. They'd just have to bung me the lolly and I'd whizz off down the shops and have a whale of a time.'

'I bet you would,' said Cam.

Then Maxy started scratching at my door

and whining and complaining. I told him to push off, because Cam and I were In Conference, but he didn't take any notice.

'Miss, Miss, it's not fair, them big girls won't let me have a go on the tape, I want a go, Miss, you tell them to let me have a go, they're playing they're pop stars, Miss, and *I* want a go.'

Cam smiled and sighed, looking at her watch.

'I'd better go back downstairs. I've got to be going in a minute anyway.'

'Oh that's not fair! Aren't you staying? You can have lunch with us lot, Jenny won't mind, and it's hamburgers on Saturday.'

'No, I'm meeting someone for lunch in the town.'

'Oh. Where are you going then?'

'Well, we'll probably have a drink and then we'll have a salad or something. My friend fusses about her figure.'

'Who wants boring old salad? If I was having lunch out I'd go to McDonald's. I'd have a Big Mac and french fries and a strawberry milkshake. See, I'm not the slightest bit institutionalized, am I?'

'You've been to McDonald's then?'

'Oh, heaps of times,' I said. And then I paused. 'Well, not actually *inside*. I was

fostered with this boring family, Julie and Ted, and I kept on at them to take me, but they said it was junk food. And I said all their boring brown beans and soggy veggy stews were the *real* junk because they looked like someone had already eaten them and sicked them up and – well, anyway, they never took me.'

'No wonder,' said Cam, grinning.

'I am allowed to go out to lunch from here, you know.'

'Are you?'

'Yes. Any day. And tell you what, I really will work on that article for you. I could work on it this week and show you what I've done. And we could discuss it. Over lunch. At McDonald's. Hint, hint, hint.'

Cam smacked the side of her head as if a great thought has just occurred to her.

'Hey, Tracy! Would you like to come out with me to McDonald's next week?'

'Yes please!' I pause. 'Really? You're not kidding?'

'Really. Next Saturday. I'll come and pick you up about twelve, OK?'

'I'll be waiting.'

And so I shall. I'd better send her a letter too, just in case she forgets.

The dumping ground.

Dear Camilla,
I'm working hard on the article.
I'll show you on Saturday. Remember we have
a lunch-date. At 12. To go to McDonald's.
From your co-writer Tracy Beaker.

P.S Goblinda says if you took her to
McDonald's she'd be ever so good and wouldn't
gob once.

I know she said twelve o'clock. And she's not exactly the most punctual of people. She mightn't get here till ten past. Even twenty or half past. So why am I sitting here staring out of the window when we've only just had breakfast?

I hate waiting. It really gets on my nerves. I can't concentrate on anything. Not even my writing. And I haven't done any writing in this book all week because I've been so busy with my article for Cam. I've got it all finished now and even though I say it myself I've done a really great job. She can just bung it at her editor and no-one will be any the wiser. I should really get the whole fee for it myself. But I'm very generous. I'll share fifty fifty with Cam, because she's my friend.

Old Pete's my friend too. We've been bumping into each other in the middle of the night this week, on a sheet sortie. Mostly we just had a little whisper but last night I found him all huddled up and soggy because he'd had a nightmare about his nan. Strangely enough, I'd had a nightmare about my mum and it had brought on a bad attack of my hay fever. Normally I like to keep to myself at such moments as some stupid ignorant twits think my red eyes and runny nose are because I've

been crying. And I never *ever* cry, no matter what.

But I knew Peter wouldn't tease me so I huddled down beside him for a bit and when I felt him shivering I put my arm round him and told him he was quite possibly my best friend ever.

He's just come up to me now and asked if I want to play paper games. Yeah, it might pass the time.

_ A _ I L L A   L A _ _ O N

B K U D E Y J P T R Y

Oh charming! Peter and I had just got started and I was about to win the first game when Elaine the Pain comes buzzing in. She's here dumping off some boring new kid and now she wants to have a little chat with Peter.

'Well, tough, Elaine, because *I'm* having a little chat with Peter right now,' I said.

'Now now Tracy,' said Elaine.

'Yes, *now*,' I said.

Elaine bared her teeth at me. That smile means she'd really like to give me a clip around the ear but she's going to make allowances for me.

'I expect you're feeling a bit het up this morning, Tracy, because of this writer coming to take you out. Jenny's told me all about it. It'll be a lovely treat for you.'

'You bet. And it'll be a lovely treat for her too because I've written this article for her.'

'Well, I might have a little treat up my sleeve for Peter here,' Elaine said, and she shuffled him off into a corner and started talking to him earnestly.

She's still talking to him. She's keeping her voice down. But I can have very large waggly ears when I want. Elaine's going on about these people she knows. An older couple whose children have all grown up. And now they're a bit lonely. They'd like to look after

127

someone. A little boy. Maybe a little boy just like Peter.

So that's it. Little Peetie-Weetie is obviously going to get fostered and live Happily Ever After.

Well, that's good, isn't it? Because he's my best friend.

No, it's bad, because he won't be able to be my best friend any more if he goes off and gets himself fostered.

And it's not fair. He's hardly been here any time. I've been here ages and ages and no-one ever wants to foster me now.

Still, who wants to be fostered by some boring older couple anyway? Older might mean really ancient. And crabby. And strict. They'd never wear jeans or write funny letters or take Peter to McDonald's.

I wish Cam would hurry up and come for me. Although it's nowhere near time. It's daft me sitting here by the window like this. Waiting.

Justine is hovering behind me. I think she's waiting for her dad. I hope she won't tell him about the little accident to her Mickey Mouse clock. He might come and beat me up. Even though the clock's all mended now. Jenny took it in to this shop and they sorted it. I was glad to see old Mickey tick-tocking round and round again. Justine caught me looking

128

and she gave me this great fierce push that nearly knocked me over and told me that if I so much as touched her clock again she'd duff me up good and proper. Honestly! My fists clenched and I was all set to have a real go at her because no-one talks to Tracy Beaker like that, but then I remembered my lunch date. Jenny isn't best pleased with me at the moment. If I got into a punch-up with Justine then she mightn't let me go out with Cam.

So I Kept Calm. I smiled at Justine in a superior sort of way.

'Really Justine, do you always have to resort to violence?' I said.

My superior willpower was wasted on Justine. She just thought I was chicken.

'Cowardy cowardy custard,' she's mumbling under her breath now. 'Tracy Beaker's got no bottle.'

I shan't take any notice of her. I shall just sit here writing. And waiting. It's not *that* long now. Only it seems like for ever.

I used to sit like this. When I waited for my mum. I wonder when she will come. I had that awful dream about her. I was out having lunch with Cam in McDonald's and it was really great and we were having a smashing time together when I looked up at the clock and saw it had gone one o'clock, and

it suddenly rang a terrible bell in my head, and I remembered that my mum was coming to take me to lunch at one o'clock, and I just went panic panic panic.

I charged off to try to get back to the Home in time and I got a bus but they chucked me off because I didn't have enough money and then I ran into Aunty Peggy and she chased after me to give me a good smacking and Julie and Ted tripped me up and Justine caught me and threw me in a river and I couldn't swim and I was drowning . . . and then I woke up. Wet.

So OK, I know it was only a dopey old nightmare. But what if it was some kind of *premonition*??? What if my mum really comes for me today and I miss her because I'm having lunch with Cam?

I'll have to talk to Elaine.

Well, I've talked. Sort of.

'Can I have a little chat, Elaine?' I said.

'Tracy. I'm still having a little chat with Peter.'

'You've *had* a little chat with Peter. Correction. You've had an extremely long and boring endless conversation with him. And you're my social worker just as much as his. So could you *please* come and have a little chat with me. It's sort of urgent.'

Elaine sighed. She ruffled Peter's hair and gave him a little chuck under the chin. Then she came over to me at long last.

'What is it then, Tracy?'

I swallowed, not sure how to put it.

'Tracy, are you just winding me up?' said Elaine.

'No! It's just . . . Look, about my mum. She doesn't know I'm here, does she?'

'Well. No, I don't think so.'

'But if she wanted to find me she could, couldn't she?'

I said it in a whisper but Justine heard.

131

'Who'd ever want to come looking for you, Tracy Beaker?' she said.

'You shut your mouth!'

Justine pulled a hideous face and Louise giggled. Then she tugged at Justine's sleeve.

'Come on. Let's see what that new girl's doing. She's got two whole suitcases with her, so she must have heaps of clothes.'

But Justine wanted to stay at the window so Louise wandered off by herself. I knew Justine was still listening for all she was worth (honestly, some people have no decency whatsoever) but I had to keep on asking Elaine.

'If my mum wanted she could go round to that old children's home. And they could tell her where I am now, couldn't they?'

'Yes, of course they would,' said Elaine. 'Don't worry, Tracy. Each time you get moved on somewhere else, there's a special record kept. So if your mum wants to see you then it's easy. They look up your name and file number and find your present address.'

'Good,' I said.

'What's up, Tracy? You still look a bit worried.'

'I'm OK.'

Only I don't feel OK. What if my mum does come today? And I'm out having lunch with someone else? Will she wait for me? Or

132

will she get fidgety and fed up and zoom off again? And I'll get back here and Jenny will say, 'Oh, by the way, Tracy, your mum called when you were out, but she couldn't wait for you. She was all set to take you back to Hollywood with her but she had this plane to catch so she couldn't hang about.'

What am I going to do?

Maybe she won't come today. She hasn't ever come before. And yet, what if she did? I *wish* I hadn't had that dream. Dreams *can* come true.

I feel sick. Maybe I don't really want to go to McDonald's after all.

See that? It's real blood.

I'm not going to get to go to McDonald's now, whether I want to or not. I've had a fight. I'm in the Quiet Room.

This is how it happened. I went over to Peter. I whispered in his ear.

'Would you like to go to McDonald's with Cam?'

Peter scrunched up his neck because my whispers can be a bit tickly.

'You mean, go with you?'

'No. Go instead of me. I've kind of gone off the idea. It's OK, I'll tell Cam when she comes. She quite likes you, so she won't mind taking you instead.'

Peter looked worried.

'I can't, Tracy. I'm going out too. With these people.'

'What, with this boring older couple?' I said.

Elaine raised her eyebrows at me but I took no notice.

'I bet they won't take you to McDonald's,' I said.

'Why don't *you* want to go, Tracy?' Elaine asked. 'I thought you were so looking forward to it.'

'Yes, but ... I want to stay here. Just in case.'

Elaine is a pain but she's also quite quick at putting two and two together.

'Tracy, I don't think your mum will be coming today,' she said quietly.

'Oh. I know that. Only I had this dream. She did in the dream.'

'Yes, I'm sure she did. And I expect it was a lovely dream but—'

'No, it was a perfectly foul dream because I wasn't here to see her and—'

'And you woke up blubbing with a soaking wet bed, *baby*,' Justine muttered.

'I told you to shut *up*,' I said, getting really riled.

'I'd go out with your writer friend, Tracy,' said Elaine.

'Mm. Well. I'm not sure I really want to now, anyway.' I glare at Peter. 'Why do you have to be seeing this boring old couple today, eh? You could see them any old time. You go and have a Big Mac with Cam.'

Peter wriggled. Elaine put her hand on his shoulder. He looked up at her and then at me.

'Sorry, Tracy. I want to meet them. Aunty Vi and Uncle Stanley.'

'Of course you want to meet them, Peter. And Tracy is going to meet her writer,' said Elaine.

'No, I'm not.'

'*I'd* go,' said Justine. 'Only I can't, because of my dad. I'm going out to lunch with him.'

'You were supposed to be going out with him last Saturday. Only he never turned up,' I said.

'OK, but he does come *sometimes*. Not like your famous mum. She's never ever ever come for you,' said Justine.

'Oh yes she has!' I yelled. 'She's come for me lots of times. She's going to come and take me away for good, we're going to Hollywood

together and – will you stop *laughing* at me, you great big pig.'

'You're so stupid,' Justine gasped. 'Your mum's not a film star. Louise told me about your mum. She's nothing. And she's never coming for you. She hasn't been near you since you were little. I bet she's forgotten all about you. Or she's had heaps of other kids and doesn't want to think about that boring ugly Tracy ever again.'

So I hit her. And I kept on hitting her. And I don't care. I've made her nose bleed again. She's hurt me a bit too, but I don't care. And now I'm stuck in the Quiet Room and it's gone twelve and one of the other kids will get to go out to lunch with Cam instead of me and I don't care. At least it won't be Justine.

Maybe my mum *will* come.

There's someone outside the door. It's opening. *Is it Mum???*

No. It wasn't Mum. It never is. It was Cam, of course.

I took one look at Cam and burst into tears. Well, I would have done, if I was a crying sort of person.

'Oh dear,' said Cam. 'I don't seem to have a very good effect on you, Tracy.'

She sat right down on the floor beside me, waiting for me to quieten down a bit. Then she dug in the pocket of her jeans and found a crumpled tissue. She passed it to me and I mopped up my hay fever.

'Now,' said Cam. 'What do you want to do?'

'I haven't got any choice, have I? I'm stuck here.'

'No you're not. You can still come out to lunch with me. I've asked Jenny. Elaine explained why you got upset.'

'She doesn't know! I hate the idea of you lot all blabbing away about me,' I said fiercely.

'Yes, it must get a bit annoying,' said Cam. 'Still, at least it means you're the centre of everyone's attention. Here, you've still got a runny nose. Good job you weren't wearing your make-up this time.'

'Are you laughing at me?'

'Just a little tease. Coming?'

'You bet.'

Only I *still* felt bothered about my mum, even though I knew it was silly. I knew she almost definitely wouldn't be coming. I knew deep deep down that Justine was maybe right about her. But I still worried.

'My mum,' I mumbled.

'You're scared she'll come and you won't be here?' said Cam. 'OK. Tell you what we'll do. You can phone home when we're out. To check she's not arrived. And if she *has* I'll whisk you straight back. How about that?'

'That sounds great,' I said.

So Cam and I went off together for our lunch appointment after all. She's got this ancient grass-green Citroën which made a bit of a change from the Minivan.

'My mum wouldn't be seen dead in this sort of naff car,' I said. 'She drives a Cadillac you know.'

'Mm,' said Cam.

I squinted at her. 'You're just nodding to
be nice to me, aren't you?' I said. 'You don't
really believe my mum's got her own Cadillac.'

Cam looked at me. 'Do you believe it,
Tracy?'

I thought for a bit. 'Sometimes.'

Cam nodded again.

'And sometimes I know I'm sort of making it
up,' I mumbled. 'Do you mind that? Me telling
lies?'

'I make things up all the time when I
write stories. I don't mind a bit,' said Cam.

'I've got that article with me. I've written
it all. You won't have to bother with a thing.
Shall I read a bit to you? You'll be really
impressed, I bet you will. I think I've done
a dead professional job.'

So I started reading it to her.

'You can see the signs of suffering on little Tracy Beaker's elfin face. This very very intelligent and extremely pretty little girl has been grievously treated when in so-called Care. Her lovely talented young mother had to put her in a home through no fault of her own, and in fact she might soon be coming for her lovely little daughter, but until then dear little Tracy Beaker needs a foster family. She is deprived and abused in the dump of a children's home— Why are you laughing, Cam?'

'Abused?' Cam spluttered.

'Look at my hand. My knuckles. That's blood, you know.'

'Yes, and you got it bouncing your fist up and down on poor Justine's nose,' said Cam. 'You're the one who deprives and abuses all the others in your Home.'

'Yes, but if I put that no-one will want me, will they?'

'I don't know,' said Cam. 'If I were choosing, I'd maybe go for a really naughty girl. It might be fun.'

I looked at her. And went on looking at her. And my brain started going tick tick tick.

I was mildly distracted when we got to McDonald's. I ate a Big Mac and a large portion of french fries, and washed it down with a strawberry milkshake. So did Cam. Then she had a coffee and I had another milkshake. And then we sat back, stuffed. We both had to undo our belts a bit.

I got out my article again and showed her some more, but she got the giggles all over again.

'I'll give myself hiccups,' she said weakly. 'It's no use, Tracy. I think it's great, but they'll never print it. You can't say those sort of things.'

'What, that Tracy Beaker is brilliant and the best child ever? It's true!'

'Maybe! But you can't say all the other things, about Justine and Louise and the rest.'

'But they're true too.'

'No, they're not true at all. I've met them. I like them. And you certainly can't say those things about Jenny and Mike and your social worker and all the others. You'd get sued for libel.'

'Well, you do better then,' I said huffily. 'What would you put?'

'I don't know. Maybe I don't want to do the article now anyway. I think I'd sooner stick to my stories, and blow the money.'

'That's not a very professional approach,' I said sternly. 'Maybe you ought to give up writing. Maybe you ought to do some job that gives you a whacking great allowance. Looking after someone. You get an allowance for that.'

Cam raised her eyebrows.

'I can barely look after myself,' she said.

'Well then. You need someone to look after you for a bit,' I said. 'Someone like me.'

'Tracy.' Cam looked me straight in the eye. 'No. Sorry. *I* can't foster you.'

'Yes, you can.'

'Stop it. We can't start this. I'm not in any position to foster you.'

'Yes you are. You don't need to be married, you know. Single women can foster kids easy-peasy.'

142

'I'm single and I want to stay single. No husband. And *no kids*.'

'Good. I hate other kids. Especially boring little babies. You won't ever get broody, will you, Cam?'

'No fear. Holding that little Wayne was enough to douse any maternal urges for ever,' said Cam.

'So it could be just you and me.'

'No!'

'Think about it.'

Cam laughed. 'You aren't half persistent, girl! OK, OK, I'll think about it. That's all. Right?'

'Right,' I say, and I tap her hand triumphantly. 'Can I phone home now? I sound like E.T., don't I? We've got through two videos of that already. So, can T.B. phone home? Only she doesn't have any change.'

Cam gave me ten pence and I went to the phone by the Ladies and gave Jenny a buzz. My heart did thump a bit when I was waiting for her to answer. I felt a little bit sad when she told me that Mum hadn't come. Even though that was the answer I was really expecting.

But I had other things to fuss about now. I whizzed back to Cam.

'Well? Have you had your think? Is it

OK? Will you take me on?' I asked eagerly.

'Hey, hey! I've got to think about this for ages and ages. And then I'm almost certain it's still going to be no.'

'*Almost* certain. But not absolutely one hundred percent.'

'Mm. What about you? Are you absolutely one hundred percent sure you'd like me to foster you?'

'Well. I'd sooner you were rich. And posh and that, so that I could get on in the world.'

'I think you'll get on in the world without my help, Tracy.'

'No, I need you, Cam.'

I looked straight at her. And she looked straight at me.

'We still hardly know each other,' she said.

'Well, if we lived together we would get to know each other, wouldn't we, Cam? Camilla. That sounds classier. I want my foster mum to sound dead classy.'

'Oh Tracy, give it a rest. Me, classy? And I told you, I can't stick Camilla. I used to get teased. And that's what my mum always called me.' She pulled a face.

I was shocked by her tone and her expression.

'Don't you ... don't you *like* your mum?' I said.

'Not much.'

'Why? Did she beat you up or something?'

'No! No, she just bossed me about. And my father too. They tried to make me just like them and when I wanted to be different they couldn't accept it.'

'So don't you see them any more?'

'Not really. Just at Christmas.'

'Good, so they'll give me Christmas presents, won't they, if I'm their foster grandchild?'

'Tracy! Look, it really wouldn't work. It wouldn't work for heaps of practical reasons, let alone anything else. I haven't got room for you. I live in this tiny flat.'

'I'm quite small. I don't take up much space.'

'But my flat's really minute, you should see it.'

'Oh great! Can we go there now?'

'I didn't mean—' Cam began – but she laughed again. 'OK, we'll go round to my flat. Only I told Jenny I'd take you back to the Home after lunch.'

'T.B. can phone home again, can't she?'

'I suppose so. Tell Jenny I'll get you back by teatime.'

'Can't I come to tea with you too? Please?'

'Tell you what. We could pretend to be posh ladies just to please you and have afternoon tea. About four. Although I don't know how either of us could possibly eat another thing.

And then I'll take you back to the Home by five. Right?'

'What about supper? And look, I could stay the night, we're allowed to do that, and I don't need pyjamas, I could sleep in my underwear, and I needn't bother about washing things, I often don't wash back at the Home—'

'Great! Well, if you ever lived with me – and I said *if*, Tracy – then you'd wash all right. Now don't carry on. Five. Back at the Home. That'll be quite enough for today.'

I decided to give in. I sometimes sense I can only push so far.

I phoned, and Cam spoke to Jenny for a bit too.

'T.B.'s phoned home twice now. Like E.T. Do you know what E.T. got?' I said hopefully. 'Smarties.'

'You'll be in the Sunday papers tomorrow, Tracy. THE GIRL WHOSE STOMACH EXPLODED,' said Cam.

But she bought me Smarties all the same. Not a little tube, a great big packet.

'Wow! Thanks,' I said, tucking in.

'They're not just for you. Take them back and share them with all the others.'

'Oh! I don't want to waste them.'

'You're to share them, greedyguts.'

'I don't mind sharing them with Peter. Or Maxy. Or the babies.'

'Share them with everybody. Including Justine.'

'Hmm!'

She stopped off at another shop too. A baker's. She made me wait outside. She came out carrying a cardboard box.

'Is that cakes for our tea?'

'Maybe.'

'Yum yum. I'm going to like living with you, Cam.'

'Stop it now. Look Tracy, I seem to have got a bit carried away. I like seeing you and I hope we can go out some other Saturdays— '

'Great! To McDonald's? Is that a promise?'

'That really is a promise. But about fostering . . . I'd hate you to build your hopes up, Tracy. Let's drop the subject now and just be friends, OK?'

'You could be my friend *and* my foster mum.'

'You're like a little dog with a bone. You just won't let go, will you?'

'Woof woof!'

I'm getting good at making her laugh. I like her. Quite a lot. Not as much as my mum, of course. But she'll do, until my mum comes to get me.

Her flat came as a bit of a shock, mind you. It really is weeny. And ever so shabby. It's in far worse nick than the Home. And you should see her bedroom. She leaves her pyjamas on the floor too!

Still, once I get to live there I'll get her sorted out. Help her make a few improvements.

'Show me your books then,' I said, going over to the shelves. 'Did you write all this lot?'

'No, no! Just the ones on the bottom shelf. I don't think you'll find them very exciting, Tracy.'

She was dead right there. I flicked through one, but I couldn't find any pictures, or any funny bits, or even any rude bits. I'll have to get her to write some better books or she'll never make enough money to keep me in the style to which I want to become accustomed.

Maybe I'll have to hurry up and get my own writing published. I got Cam to give me a good long go on her typewriter.

It took me a while to get the hang of it. But eventually I managed to tap out a proper letter. I left it tucked away on Cam's desk for her to find later.

```
     DEAR CAM,   I WILL BE THE BESTEST FOSTER
CHILD EVER.   YOU'LL SEE.   WITH LOVE FROM
TRACY BEAKER, THE GIRL WHOSE STOMACH DIDN'T
EXPLODE.
```

It did nearly though. Guess what she bought for tea! A birthday cake, quite a big one, with jam and cream inside. The top

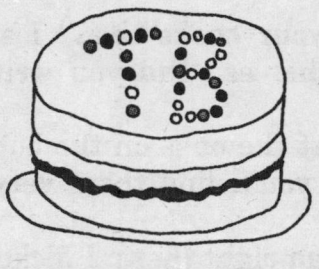

was just plain white, but she took some of my Smarties and spelt out T.B. on the top.

'So that it's all my cake,' I said happily.

'Aren't I going to get a slice?' asked Cam.

'Oh yes. Of course. But I don't have to share it with anyone else. I had to share my proper birthday cake with Peter, wasn't that *mean!*'

'I thought Peter's your friend.'

'Well. He is. But still. You don't want to share your birthday cake even with your bestest friend ever,' I said.

Only I started thinking about it all the time I was chomping my way through my first great big slice. And my second slice with extra jam and cream. And my third weeny slice. And my nibbles at a bit of icing.

'This is much better than that birthday cake at the Home, you know,' I said.

'Good.'

'Peter's gone out with this dumb sounding old auntie and uncle today,' I said.

'Has he?'

'But I bet they won't take him to Mc-Donald's. Or buy him his own special cake.'

'Maybe not.'

'Well, seeing as we are friends, Peter and me, and we share a birthday, and we shared that other birthday cake – maybe we *ought* to share this one too,' I said. 'Shall I take a slice back for my friend Peter?'

'I think that would be a good idea,' said Cam. 'I'll wrap up a slice for Peter. And another slice for you. Just so long as you promise me you won't throw up all night.'

'Of course I won't. Here, can I do the cutting this time? Because if this is like a birthday cake I get a wish, don't I?'

So Cam gave me the knife and I closed my eyes and wished really really hard.

'I bet you can't guess what I wished,' I said to Cam.

'I bet I can,' said Cam.

'I'll tell you if you like.'

'Oh no. You're supposed to keep birthday cake wishes secret,' said Cam.

I pulled a little face at her. Then I thought.

'Here, if this is a sort of birthday, then it's a pity there aren't any presents too.' I paused. 'Hint hint hint.'

'Do you know what you are, Tracy Beaker? Absolutely shameless.'

But it worked!

Cam looked all round her room and stared for a while at her bookshelves. I thought I was going to end up with a boring old book. But it was much much better. She went to her desk and picked up her Mickey Mouse pen.

'Here we are, Tracy. Happy Unbirthday,' she said, and she pressed the pen into my hand.

Just for a moment I was lost for words. And that doesn't happen very often to me. I was scared I might even get another attack of my hay fever. But I managed to grin and give her the thumbs up sign and show her that I was ever so pleased.

We got back to the Home at five. On the dot. Trust her to be punctual at the wrong time. I made a bit of a fuss on the doorstep. I sort

of clung a bit. It was just that I was enjoying myself so much that I wanted to go *on* enjoying myself. That's not being difficult, is it?

But it's still OK. She's coming next Saturday. She's promised. Twelve o'clock. We have a date, me and my future foster mum. I'm going to make that wish come true.

It took me a bit of time to calm down after we'd said goodbye. I missed out on tea, but it didn't really matter, seeing as I'd had more than half my cake and the McDonald's lunch and the Smarties. There were still quite a few Smarties left. Just no red ones. Or pink or mauve or blue. They're my favourite colours. But there were plenty of the boring ones to share with the others.

When I came out of the Quiet Room I collected my Smarties and the two slices of cake. They'd got a bit squashed as I was saying goodbye to Cam, but Jenny helped me spruce them up a bit and put them on a plate.

I went to find Peter. He was up in his room, sitting on his bed, looking a bit quiet.

'Oh oh,' I said. 'This older couple. They didn't turn up?'

'Oh yes. They did,' said Peter.

'But they were pretty awful, yes? Never you mind, Pete, see what I've got for us? Look, really yummy cake.'

'Thank you, Tracy,' said Peter, and he took his slice absent-mindedly. 'No, they aren't awful, Auntie Vi and Uncle Stanley. They're nice, actually.'

'I bet they didn't take you to McDonald's.'

'No, we went and had fish and chips. My nan and I always used to go and have fish and chips. With bread and butter and a cup of tea.'

'Boring! I had a Big Mac and french fries and a strawberry milkshake, two actually, and then Cam bought me these Smarties and then she bought me this really incredible cake and even put my name on the top. It was my extra special cake and I could have eaten it all up myself but I asked her to save a big slice for

154

you. So I did. And you haven't even started on it yet. Don't you like it? It was meant to be your big treat.'

'Oh, it's lovely, Tracy,' said Peter, munching politely. 'It's ever so good of you. I told Auntie Vi and Uncle Stanley all about you and said that you were my best friend. They want to meet you very much.'

'Well, it's no use them getting interested in me. I'm going to be fostered by Cam, you wait and see.'

'Really? That's wonderful. You see, I think Auntie Vi and Uncle Stanley want to foster me, Tracy. That's what they said. They want to take me almost straight away.'

'So you're zooming off and leaving me in this dump, are you?' I said. 'Terrific!'

'Well. I don't *want* to leave you, Tracy. I told them that. But if you're going to be fostered too . . .'

'Yeah, yeah, well Cam's desperate to have me, but you shouldn't always rush into these things you know, Peter. You should think it over carefully.'

'I know. That's what I've been trying to do,' said Peter. 'Tracy. No matter who fosters me, who fosters you, we can still stay best friends, can't we? And visit each other lots? And write letters?'

'I'll write you letters with my very own

special Mickey Mouse pen. Want to see it?'

'Oh Tracy, you didn't nick it from Cam, did you?'

'Cheek! What do you take me for? She gave it to me, dumbo. I told you she's dotty about me. OK, we'll make a pact. We'll stay best friends no matter what. Here, you're leaving all the icing. Don't you like it?'

'Well, I was saving the best bit till last. But you have it, Tracy. I want you to have it, really.'

It's quite good, sharing a cake with your best friend.

Then I went round the whole Home with the packet of Smarties. I gave one each to everyone. I even gave one to Louise and the new girl. They were upstairs together, trying on the new girl's clothes.

Justine was downstairs. At the window. Her dad hadn't turned up. She had a new sticking plaster on her face. She was sniffling.

I looked at her. My heart started going thump thump thump. I went up to her. She turned round, looking all hopeful. She thought I was Louise. But it looks like Louise might have a new best friend now. Louise is like that.

Justine jumped a bit when she saw it was me.

'What do you want, Tracy Beaker?' she mumbled, wiping her eyes.

'I've got something for you, Justine,' I said.

I thought I was going to give her a Smartie. But you'll never guess what I did. I gave her my Mickey Mouse pen.

I must be stark staring bonkers. I hope Cam can get me another one. Next Saturday. When I see her. When she tells me that she's thought it all over and she wants to be my foster mum.

This started like a fairy story. And it's going to finish like one too. Happily Ever After.

ABOUT THE AUTHOR

JACQUELINE WILSON was born in Bath in 1945, but has spent most of her life in Kingston-on-Thames, Surrey. She always wanted to be a writer and wrote her first 'novel' when she was nine, filling countless Woolworths' exercise books as she gew up. She started work at a publishing company and then went on to work as a journalist on *Jackie* magazine (which was named after her) before turning to writing fiction full-time.

Since 1990 Jacqueline has written prolifically for children and has won many of the UK's top awards for children's books, including the Smarties Prize in 2000 and the Guardian Children's Fiction Award and the Children's Book of the Year in 1999. Jacqueline was awarded an OBE in the Queen's Birthday Honours list, in Golden Jubilee Year, 2002.

Over 10 million copies of Jacqueline's books have now been sold in the UK and approximately 50,000 copies of her books are sold each month. An avid reader herself, Jacqueline has a personal collection of more than 15,000 books.

She has one grown-up daughter.

'A brilliant young writer of wit and subtlety whose stories are never patronising and are often complex and many-layered'
THE TIMES

'Jacqueline Wilson has a rare gift for writing lightly and amusingly about emotional issues'
BOOKSELLER

'Wilson writes like a child, and children instantly recognize themselves in her characters. The tone of voice is faultless, her stories are about the problems many children face, and her plots work with classic simplicity . . . a subtle art is concealed by alertness, and some might call that genius'
DAILY TELEGRAPH

Now flip the book to read

The WORRY Website